"There's One Part Of This Job We Haven't Discussed."

"Which is?"

"Sex."

"Ah," Lucius said. An expression came into his eyes, one that had her throat going dry and a hot pool of want forming in her belly. Waves of it lapped outward, roiling and seething in endless demand. "How could I have neglected something so vital?"

"I gather that's a yes."

"No."

She stiffened, shocked by his answer. Had she miscalculated? Had he considered their kiss a mild and forgettable flirtation, easily forgotten and dismissed, while she'd built it up into something far more serious and memorable?

"Not a yes?" she asked faintly.

"Not a yes," he responded gravely, "but rather a *hell* yes."

* * *

Dear Reader,

More Than Perfect brings together two people who have experienced betrayal and must learn to trust again. Add to the mix a baby in desperate need of a mother and father, and you end up with one of my favorite types of books to write—one that is emotional, has a touch of humor and deals with issues from the past that must be overcome.

Trust is one of my favorite themes to explore because so many of us have trust issues. We've all been let down by those we love and must decide to either keep our hearts tucked safely away, or take that leap of faith. I've always chosen to try one more time, to take the risk and hope that somehow, someway everything will work out. So, it never fails to delight me when love overcomes the scars and pain from the past.

For those of you with scars, I wish healing. For those wondering whether or not to take the plunge again, I hope you'll go for it. And for those of you who've risked everything, I wish you the ultimate success…love.

Warmly,

Day Leclaire

DAY
LECLAIRE

MORE THAN PERFECT

ISBN-13: 978-0-373-73152-7

MORE THAN PERFECT

This edition published by arrangement with Harlequin Books S.A.

For questions and comments about the quality of this book please contact us at Customer_eCare@Harlequin.ca.

www.Harlequin.com

Printed in U.S.A.

Recent books by Day Leclaire

Harlequin Desire

**Dante's Honor-Bound Husband* #2087
(Gianna and Constantine's story)
Nothing Short of Perfect #2121
More Than Perfect #2139

†The Royals
*The Dante Legacy

Other titles by this author available in ebook format

Silhouette Desire

†*The Forbidden Princess* #1780
†*The Prince's Mistress* #1786
†*The Royal Wedding Night* #1792
The Billionaire's Baby Negotiation #1821
**Dante's Blackmailed Bride* #1852
(Severo and Francesca's story)
**Dante's Stolen Wife* #1870
(Marco and Caitlyn's story)
**Dante's Wedding Deception* #1880
(Nicolò and Kiley's story)
**Dante's Contract Marriage* #1899
(Lazzaro and Ariana's story)
Mr. Strictly Business #1921
Inherited: One Child #1953
Lone Star Seduction #1983
**Dante's Ultimate Gamble* #2017
(Luciano and Téa's story)
**Dante's Temporary Fiancée* #2037
(Rafaelo and Larkin's story)
**Dante's Marriage Pact* #2057
(Draco and Shayla's story)
Claimed: The Pregnant Heiress #2060

DAY LECLAIRE

USA TODAY bestselling author Day Leclaire is described by Harlequin Books as "one of our most popular writers ever!" Day's tremendous worldwide popularity has made her a member of Harlequin's "Five Star Club," with sales of well over five million books. She is a three-time winner of both a Colorado Award of Excellence and a Golden Quill Award. She's won *RT Book Reviews* Career Achievement and Love and Laughter Awards, a Holt Medallion and a Booksellers' Best Award. She has also received an impressive ten nominations for the prestigious Romance Writers of America's RITA® Award.

Day's romances touch the heart and make you care about her characters as much as she does. In Day's own words, "I adore writing romances, and can't think of a better way to spend each day." For more information, visit Day at her website, www.dayleclaire.com.

To friends and family
who have been with me from the beginning.
My thanks and my love.

Prologue

He awoke to soft morning light and an empty bed.

Lucius Devlin turned his head toward the subtle indent where Lisa should have been…and wasn't. In the distance, he caught the soft murmur of her voice and couldn't quite decide if he felt relief or regret that she hadn't left.

Last night had been a mistake. A bad one.

He rolled off the mattress and crossed to his dresser. In the bottom drawer he found an old pair of drawstring sweatpants and yanked them on before heading to the kitchen. Lisa was there and at his appearance, she ended her call and flipped her cell phone closed. She sat at the table, wearing her red power suit from the day before, a cup of freshly made coffee resting at her elbow. Thank God she'd made coffee. Right now he needed it almost as desperately as he needed air to breathe.

She regarded him with eyes every bit as dark as his own while he filled a sturdy mug to the brim. "You're dressed," he said, stating the obvious. He took a swift, settling hit of caffeine, his eyes narrowing at her through the haze of steam. "I gather you're leaving?"

"Yes." She played with her cell phone with long, supple fingers and actually allowed a slight frown to crease the space between her winged brows. Damn. If she were risking wrinkles, that meant it was serious. "I am leaving, this time for good."

"Or until you and Geoff have another fight?" He gestured toward her phone. "I'm guessing he called."

Her mouth tightened a fraction. "You always were too smart for your own good."

"That makes two of us."

Lisa sighed. Leaning back in her chair, she crossed her spectacular legs and eyed him with reluctant amusement. "Why couldn't you have been a stupid billionaire and made the incredible mistake of marrying me when we were first together?"

He took her question at face value. "Probably because *stupid* and *billionaire* are incongruous since I wouldn't be a billionaire for long if I were stupid."

"That's true in your case." She tilted her head to one side, her gaze watchful. "I'm not sure you can say the same about Geoff."

Great. Now she'd forced him into the bizarre position of defending his best friend to the woman who'd slept with them both—first with him, then when he wouldn't stick a ring on her finger, she'd moved on to Geoff, the head of his PR department at Diablo, Inc. Lucius suspected it was a foolish attempt to force a proposal out of him, one that had proved a spectacular failure.

"Geoff is neither a billionaire, nor stupid," Lucius informed her. "Naive, perhaps, especially when it comes to women like you. But he's solid gold."

"Unlike us?" She didn't need his silence to confirm her question. She already knew the answer. She picked up her cup and took a dainty sip. "He's an angel with two devils sitting on his shoulders, poor boy. Would you care to place a small wager on which devil he'll listen to, Lucius? Which devil he'll obey?"

He refused to participate in whatever game Lisa seemed intent on playing. "What do you want?"

"From you? Nothing."

"And from Geoff?"

She offered a catlike smile, full of sly confidence. "I have what I want from him, as well."

Lucius stiffened, something in her tone warning of incoming mortar fire and he braced himself for the hit. "Which is?"

"A marriage proposal." Her smile grew. "That was Geoff on the phone. He's seen the error of his ways and asked me to hop on the next plane to Vegas with him. We'll be married this afternoon and on our honeymoon by tonight."

The words pounding through Lucius's brain were coarse and crude enough that he refused to speak them aloud, even in front of Lisa. "Fast work. You roll out of one man's bed one night and into another's the next, then back again on the third." He tilted his head to one side in consideration. "I think there's a name for that…."

Her smile died and her dark eyes swam with accusation and fury. "At least when I roll back into Geoff's bed I'll be wearing a wedding ring. That's more than you ever offered."

"And if I call and tell him where you were last night?"

"He already knows. Why do you think he proposed?"

For the first time he caught a crack in her legendary

control. "I'm sure you'll be relieved to hear he forgives me. Forgives us both."

This time Lucius did swear aloud. "Don't do this, Lisa. He won't survive marriage to you. You'll eat him alive."

And maybe that's why he'd allowed her to talk him into a final fling last night, in the hopes that Geoff would hear about it and finally see Lisa for what she was. An opportunist. An amoral cat who'd bed down with anyone who could afford her price. Instead, all he'd managed to do was guarantee his best friend a marriage made in hell. Great. Just great.

"If you didn't want me with Geoff, then you should have been the one to offer marriage. But you're just too damn clever for your own good, too intent on manipulating your world and everyone in it." She shoved her porcelain cup and saucer aside with a quick little jerk. The coffee sloshed over the rim and stained the virginal white saucer in bitter darkness. "I'm marrying Geoff and that's the end of it. I can make him happy and I fully intend to."

"What do they say about the road to hell?" He snapped his fingers. "Oh, right. That smear of pavement is one long, filthy tarmac of good intentions."

"In that case, I'm going to hell, though I doubt I'm going there alone. You'll be right there beside me." She shoved back her chair and stood. To his surprise tears glittered in her eyes. "Would you like to know what's funniest of all? Geoff wants to start a family right away. It's the one thing we both agree on. I may be a gold digger, but I'm a maternal one."

A fierce wave of cynicism swept through him. "Not to mention that when your marriage bombs, that little tyke you pop out ensures nice, fat child support payments to go along with that nice, fat alimony check."

Instead of his words sending her up in flames as he expected, it cooled her. "You're a total son of a bitch, Lucius. Thanks for reminding me of that fact." She snatched up her phone, shoved it into her purse and faced him with a pride he could only admire. "And one of these days I plan to make you eat those words. I may not want Geoff the way I want you, but he's a good man. A decent man. I haven't had many of those in my life. I plan to make him very happy. Delirious, in fact. And I hope you're stuck watching us enjoy that happiness for the next fifty years. That way you can choke on it."

And with that, she swept out the door.

One

"You aren't just a devil, you're a total son of a bitch!"

Angie Colter's head jerked up at the unmistakable sound of a hand striking flesh and she swiveled to stare at the closed door of her boss's office—Lucius Devlin, owner and CEO of the Seattle based company, Diablo, Inc., a multibillion dollar business that specialized in buying and rehabbing commercial real estate. The next instant the door slammed open and Ella, the gorgeous redhead Angie had ushered in not ten minutes earlier, emerged. The woman had been Devlin's latest in a long string, lasting a full two weeks. A record breaker among the spate of women her boss had seen over the past three months.

"I don't know how you could possibly think I'd be interested in your insane proposal." With that, she swept across the plush expanse of carpet on impossibly high heels, her backside twitching out her profound irritation as she headed for the private elevators.

Okay. That was interesting and added to Angie's growing suspicion that something was up with Lucius. She hadn't figured out what, but suspected the six-month-old baby he'd received guardianship of a short three months earlier was somehow responsible. The baby, Mikey, was the son of the former head of PR for Diablo, Geoff Ridgeway. He and his wife, Lisa, had died in a train wreck in Europe shortly before Christmas, appointing Lucius the guardian of their infant son. From the moment Angie had first taken Mikey into her arms, she'd fallen in love with the little guy. Maybe it was due in part to the faint ticking of her biological clock. More likely it was those huge dark eyes staring so gravely into hers. Whatever the cause, an emotion unlike any she'd ever experienced before had fisted around her heart and refused to let go.

Angie glanced toward Lucius's office in open speculation. Initially, she'd thought her boss was searching for the perfect nanny, someone to replace the sweet-natured woman who'd accepted the job in a temporary capacity. But lately… Unable to contain her curiosity, she snatched up her electronic tablet and stylus. Crossing to the open doorway, she gave a brisk knock.

Her boss stood in profile, drowning a handful of ice cubes in scotch. Through the floor-to-ceiling windows behind him sprawled the city of Seattle, modestly veiling its beauty behind a misty, gray morning. At six foot two Lucius "The Devil" Devlin possessed a powerful physique at odds with a job that required endless hours behind a desk. No doubt he'd spent some of his billions on a home gym, filled with the best equipment money could buy. And used it with the same ruthless efficiency that characterized everything else he did in his life. He was a gorgeous man with hair the color of soot and eyes as dark and mysterious as a moonless night. A man who could steal a woman's breath without even trying. And the first time he'd tossed his devil-may-care smile in her direction, he'd stolen her heart...and quite possibly her soul.

Maybe that was why she'd committed the ultimate folly and fallen in love with him.

He glanced over his shoulder at her and frowned. "This isn't a good time."

The scowl snapped her back into focus. Ignoring his order, she stepped into the office. "Try using some of that ice on your jaw," she instructed crisply. "It'll help with the swelling."

"She packs quite a punch for a woman."

"I don't doubt it. Ella can bench-press a hundred and a quarter."

He swiveled to fully face her. "Get out. Seriously?"

"Dead serious. We go to the same gym. You're even more lucky she didn't use those Christian Louboutin heels on you. I've seen what she can do in our kickboxing class. She'd have skewered you like a shish kebab."

"She never mentioned she knew you."

Angie didn't doubt it. That would involve connecting with someone of the female sex. Ella only had eyes for men. "I doubt she noticed me. I don't exactly stand out."

Lucius tossed back the scotch, then took her suggestion and pressed the iced glass against the red mark darkening his jaw. His gaze swept over her. Even though he stripped her with that swift look, it was in a—sadly—asexual manner. Not that it surprised her. She knew what he saw. She'd come to the conclusion long ago that she had a head for business and a bod for...well, business.

At five foot eight, she was as slender as a reed, her curves best classified as subtle. Granted, she possessed an attractive enough face and great hair, even if she did keep it confined in an elegant twist, the color containing every shade of brown known to man. But her most attractive feature were her eyes, a brilliant aquamarine that her former lover had called "unnerving." Of course, that was right before he'd dumped her for her five-foot-two, blonde and buxom—*former*—best friend, whom he'd promptly married. Nine months later they produced the baby she'd dreamed of having with him, and that he'd claimed he not only didn't want, but would never want. Maybe that was why Angie had chosen to throw every scrap of her time and energy into her career. While Britt was giving birth to Ryan's baby, Angie secured the prime job as Lucius Devlin's PA. She hadn't quite decided who got the better deal, which told her that maybe her feelings for Ryan hadn't run as deep as she'd thought.

"Ella didn't notice you because you're female," Lucius stated, echoing her earlier thoughts. "Not because you don't stand out. The right clothes, the right hairstyle—"

She stiffened, pricked by his careless dissection. The hazards of loving a man who saw you as a piece of equipment rather than a human being. Damn him. Her chin shot up and she pinned him with her "unnerving" gaze, pleased to have found some use for it. "Oh, wow. Advice from Lucius 'The Devil' Devlin on how to transform myself into the perfect woman. Wait now. Let me take notes." She flipped her electronic tablet over and allowed the stylus to hover above it. "Please, Lucius. Don't keep me waiting. Other than the right clothes and hairstyle, how else am I lacking?"

"Hell, woman."

She narrowed her eyes at his use of the word *woman,* pleased to see him wince. Huh. Maybe she'd patent the look. It was certainly coming in handy. "You should know all about hell, Lucius."

A grim expression closed over his face and he snatched

up the cut glass decanter, splashing more scotch into his glass. "I should and I do."

Despite the threatening storm clouds, Angie refused to back down. "I don't doubt it." She lifted an eyebrow in open challenge. "Anything else you'd care to add about my appearance?"

He took a long swallow, regarding her over the rim of his tumbler with intense black eyes. "Not a chance."

"I didn't think so." She gestured toward his glass. "Put the ice back on your face or you'll have to explain that bruise to your clients. I shudder to think what sort of nose-dive your reputation will take when you're forced to admit you were coldcocked by a woman."

"That's not how I'm going to tell the story." Still, she couldn't help but notice that he rested the glass against his jaw—an aching jaw if she didn't miss her guess.

She offered an angelic smile. "No, but it's how I plan to tell it."

"How the hell could I have thought you'd make the perfect PA?" he snarled. "I must have been out of my mind."

"Agreed." Unable to contain her curiosity, she asked, "What in the world did you say to Ella that made her so mad?"

His annoyance intensified. "You would think it was my fault."

"Do I owe you an apology?"

She could see the internal debate rage, before he settled on admitting the truth. "No, it was my fault. I made the mistake of proposing to her."

Angie struggled to breathe. He couldn't have hit her any harder if he'd been the one doing the kickboxing. "What?"

He glanced her way and blew out a sigh. "Oh, get over it, Colter. This isn't high school. We're not talking about some grand romance. Hell, I've only known the woman for two weeks. I made a business proposition that involved marriage and for some reason that ticked her off. Go figure."

Her world righted itself and she found she could breathe again. It took a second longer to settle her face into something that passed for mild interest. Another few seconds to gain control over her vocal cords so she didn't sound as shrill as a steam whistle. Until that moment, she hadn't realized just how bad she had it, just how desperately she'd fallen for him. His brilliance. His innate kindness, a kindness he worked so hard to encase in a cold, tough exterior. The wealth of inexplicable pain buried in his eyes, and no doubt his heart. In the year and a half she'd worked for him, she'd gotten to know the man behind the reputation. And with that knowing had come the sort of love she'd only played at with Ryan, skating across the surface of the emotion without embracing the true depths and scope.

Gathering her control, she allowed a cool smile to drift across her mouth. "You're right, Lucius. I can't imagine why any woman in her right mind would find a marriage proposal phrased as a business proposition in the least offensive," she commented drily. "Go figure."

Lucius set his glass down with a decisive click that caused the ice to shiver in warning. He took a step in her direction and fixed her with a dark, impenetrable gaze. "You have an opinion to offer on the subject?"

She didn't answer the question directly, didn't dare. "Is this about Mikey?" She couldn't help the softening that came into her voice when she said the name, any more than she could help the softening that invaded her whole being when she held the baby in her arms and imagined what it would be like to have something so precious come from her own body.

He hesitated and she could tell that he wanted to rip her

apart in order to release some of his fury toward Ella. But he wasn't the type to take his aggression out on an innocent. He gathered himself, banked the fire, then nodded. "Yes," he admitted. "This is about Mikey."

"You're attempting to find someone who would make a suitable wife for you and a good mother for the baby?"

"Again, yes."

"And you expected Ella to jump at the opportunity after a two-week courtship?"

His teeth came together with a snap. "I had my reasons for believing it a distinct possibility. Are you done with the cross-examination?"

He'd reached the end of his rope and she responded accordingly. "Absolutely."

"Then may I suggest we get some work done? We still have to finalize the schedule for my meeting with Gabe Moretti."

She touched the screen of her tablet and called up the pertinent information. "He's agreed to go in on the Richter building with you?"

"Only if I give him majority interest."

"No doubt," Angie replied. "But if he remodels it the way he did Diamondt Towers, it'll be well worth the investment, even with only a minority stake."

"That's not good enough."

"No, it never is." He was a man who needed to hold the reins. Unfortunately, so was Gabe Moretti. "Will Moretti concede the point?"

"We plan to meet and discuss terms."

Meaning…no. Moretti had no intention of giving up majority interest, which suggested a showdown between titans. What she wouldn't give to see that! She touched an app on the screen that accessed Lucius's calendar. "Would you prefer a lunch meeting or dinner?"

He considered, took another sip of his refilled drink before returning it to his jaw. "Dinner on Friday. Let's make it at Milano's on the Sound. Speak to Joe personally about the menu, would you?"

She made a quick notation. "I'll take care of it. Eight o'clock work for you?"

"Only if it works for you."

Angie's poise faltered for a telling instant before she gathered herself back up. "Sorry?"

"Now that Ella's out of the picture, I'll need you to attend with me. You're one of the most observant people I know. I could use your input on this." His smile drew attention to features devil-perfect and sinfully attractive, and her heart gave a sharp, painful tug. "Problem?"

She dragged her gaze away from his dark, angel beauty and focused on the tablet, pretending to make a quick notation. "I'll check my schedule and get back to you."

"Right. You do that."

She let the hint of mockery wash over her. "Next. I have several calls from a Pretorius St. John. He indicated it was a private matter. Something about a computer program he was personalizing for you. If it isn't anything you want me to deal with, I'll forward it to your PDA."

"Go ahead and do that."

She hesitated. "That name is familiar for some reason. Should I know it?"

"It's possible. His nephew is Justice St. John, the robotics wunderkind. Pretorius specializes in computer software."

Wow. "Okay, color me impressed that you have a software inventor willing to tweak one of his programs in order to fit your personal specifications."

"You know, there are some days I think you forget who you're working for."

"Oh, dear. Not again." She made an exaggerated curtsy. "I do apologize, Mr. Devlin, sir. I promise I'll be more careful in the future."

"See that you are." His eyes glittered with laughter while he studied her, curiosity spilling into the intense darkness. "I don't intimidate you in the least, do I?"

"No."

It was the truth. For some reason he didn't and never had. That hadn't been her problem, mainly because she'd been too busy fighting her attraction for him to worry about his standing in the business community. Instead, she'd done everything within her power to conceal her reaction whenever they accidentally touched. To hide how desperately she'd like to experience his hands on her. His mouth. His body covering hers with nothing between them but the damp sheen of want. She closed her eyes briefly, closed off those sort of painful, wayward thoughts—something that grew more difficult with each passing day—and fought to regain her equilibrium.

Lucius was a closed door to her. What she felt for him would never become a reality and the sooner she accepted that fact the sooner she could move on. Only one problem with that plan. She didn't want to move on. She wanted… *him.*

To her eternal gratitude, Lucius didn't appear to notice anything wrong. "Your self-possession and your natural way of behaving around me are two of the qualities I most appreciate about you."

If he only knew. "Just two?" she managed to tease.

"Fishing for compliments, Colter?"

"You bet." She pretended to cast a fishing line and reel it in, forcing out a careless grin.

"Fair enough."

He approached, circling like a shark, unnerving her

for the first time in the eighteen months they'd worked together. Until now he'd regarded her almost like a piece of office furniture. Useful. Functional. An integral, if replaceable, cog in the wheel that was Diablo. This time when he looked at her it was through a man's eyes. Her amusement faded and it took every ounce of that self-possession he'd applauded only moments before to maintain her poise and keep a calm, cool expression on her face. Her grip tightened on the electronic tablet and stylus and she could only hope he didn't notice the whitening of her knuckles or the tension pouring off her. Though, knowing Lucius, he not only noticed but would use it against her.

"Do you know why I picked you out of all the endless candidates to be my PA?" he surprised her by asking.

"Not a clue," she admitted. "I'm good at my job, but so were the other applicants, I assume."

"You're wrong," he said softly. "You're not good. You're great."

He'd stunned her. When she'd first started working for him eighteen months ago, he'd chosen her from a pool of dozens of equally efficient and qualified PAs, women—and men—who were the best in the country. Granted, Angie had worked hard for the opportunity, particularly since she'd failed in just about every other area of her life. But Lucius Devlin could afford to hire the very best, and deep down she couldn't quite convince herself that *she* was the best. And yet, here he stood, insisting she wasn't just good, but great.

"Great," she repeated faintly.

"Don't get a swelled head, Colter. Though you were great when I interviewed you, there were others who were better."

"Then why...?" Her eyes narrowed, the truth hitting

like a tidal wave. After she'd been offered the position, she'd worked longer and harder than she thought physically possible, throwing herself into the job to justify having been chosen. No doubt that's why he'd hired her. He knew she'd go the extra distance, knew on some level she'd been desperate enough to throw her heart and soul into the position. Maybe the other women hadn't been quite as committed. The knowledge that he'd used her with such deliberation gave her heart a small, painful twist. She'd been used before by Ryan and vowed at that time to never allow it to happen again. The fact that it had been Lucius who used her hurt all the more. "Damn it, Devlin. That's low, even for you."

He picked up on her intensity, caught the ripple of pain in her soft words. "If I'd known you then as well as I know you now, I'd have chosen a different method. But I needed to work you—hard—to make sure we were a good fit." An odd expression swept through his gaze, something she couldn't quite identify, but that caused her pulse rate to kick up a notch. "And we are a good fit, aren't we, Angie?"

Her mouth tugged to one side in a reluctant smile. "So far. But if you play me like that again, we won't be any sort of fit."

"Fair enough." He shot her a quick grin. "Still, you have to admit it worked. Not only did it work, but you've more than proved yourself. You've exceeded even my high standards."

"You're welcome," she murmured drily.

"That staggering paycheck you receive is my thanks. I'll even throw in a bonus if you go out and buy something decent to wear to our dinner with Moretti. I want him so focused on you that his reputation for being all business, all the time, will take a serious beating. Thanks to you, I expect him to be less business and more man. Got it?"

"I wasn't hired for that," she retorted tightly.

"You were hired to do the jobs I assign you. That's the current job."

Now what? Did she admit that she wasn't equipped to handle the current job? Or did she simply allow him to figure that out for himself? Because there wasn't a doubt in her mind that the level of excellence she exhibited at work perfectly balanced the level of mediocrity she exhibited in every other area of her life, particularly under the heading of male-female relationships. Hadn't Ryan explained that to her in no uncertain terms when he "accidentally" tripped and fell naked on top of her best friend, Britt? And in their bed, no less. What had he told her…?

Oh, right. Though she had brains and business acumen in spades, but when it came to hearth and home—particularly the bedroom portion of the home—he found her decidedly lacking. Fair enough. She found Britt and Ryan's concept of friendship equally lacking. That's when she'd decided to stick to what she was best at…work. And she had, until she'd committed a huge error. That absolute no-no of no-nos. She'd fallen in love with the boss.

She spared Lucius a single, searing look. "I don't know how, but I fully intend to make you pay for putting me through this humiliation."

That stopped him. "You consider dinner out with your boss and a client humiliating?"

"No, I consider playing the part of a seductress for my boss and his client humiliating."

Anger flared in Lucius's dark gaze. "I don't recall saying anything about seducing Moretti. Merely distracting him."

"It's not a role I'm comfortable with. And I resent being

put in that position. You know damn well that's not part of my job description." She held up a hand before he could argue the point. "And don't try and claim my job is whatever you tell me it is. That's not going to fly with me. It's whatever you tell me within the confines of the four corners of this office building. Period."

Under any other circumstance, she would have found his look of pure masculine bewilderment and frustration amusing. Instead, it tempted her to follow Ella's example and give him a good, hard smack upside his clueless head.

"You've attended business dinners before," he protested.

"Not in the sort of role you've assigned for this one."

He tossed back the last of his scotch and set the glass down with a sharp crack. "Fine. Show up looking like a piece of office furniture if that will make you feel better."

Fury sparked, spilled over. "Office furniture?"

He stalked to the front of his desk, seized one of the twin chairs positioned there and swept it in a swift one-eighty. "Office furniture," he repeated.

It took two full seconds to make the connection, to notice the simple white cream and black speckled fabric of the chair was an almost perfect match for the simple white cream and black speckled fabric of her suit. Hot color washed into her cheeks. Dear Lord. Earlier she'd thought he saw her as little more than a piece of office equipment rather than a human being. Apparently, that office equipment was furniture. Damn it! Maybe that was because she'd turned herself into office furniture.

When she'd first started work at Diablo, she'd deliberately chosen colors and designs that would help her blend with the background. Create the appearance of the perfect PA. Clearly, she'd taken the concept a step too far. Maybe a couple of steps too far.

"Well, hell," she muttered.

"Exactly."

She considered the problem for a moment. "How about this…? If I promise not to show up wearing chair upholstery, could I just be myself?" Something flickered to life in his eyes at the question. Sympathy? Compassion? She could only hope it wasn't pity. "To be honest, I'm not cut out to play the part of Mata Hari."

He inclined his head. "Fair enough. You can leave a few hours early tomorrow in order to purchase an appropriate dress and accessories. Save your receipts and I'll reimburse the expense." He checked his watch. "Keesha is due with Mikey at four, so I'll need to have my desk cleared by then. Hold any calls unless they're urgent. Oh, and don't forget to forward the messages from Pretorius St. John."

"Already done."

He nodded in clear dismissal and Angie didn't waste any time retreating to the outer office. She crossed to an antique table that held a coffee and tea service and helped herself to a restorative cup of hot tea. She didn't know what had upset her more…Friday's dinner, the fact that she'd transformed herself into a chair or the discovery that Lucius was actively looking for a wife.

Idiot! Of course she knew which upset her more. She was totally, ridiculously in love with a man who compared her to office furniture. How would she handle it if—*when*—he found a woman willing to marry him? If she were forced, day after day to watch the two enjoying the sort of marital bliss she'd always longed to experience? She closed her eyes. She knew how she'd handle it, what she'd force herself to do if—*when*—that event occurred.

If Lucius married, Angie would quit her job.

* * *

"Pretorius? Lucius Devlin here. We have a problem."

A pained sigh slipped across the phone lines. "Don't tell me the program still isn't working."

"The program still isn't working."

"Maybe you're not waiting long enough before popping the question. How much time did you give this latest one?"

"Two weeks."

"Two…" Pretorius sputtered. "Are you nuts? No woman in her right mind is going to agree to marry you after a two-week acquaintance. Why is it that brilliant men, men who are beyond adept at conquering their small corner of the world, think every other aspect of their life should be equally as simple and straightforward. Like I told Justice, these are *women* we're talking about. Not robots. And not real estate."

"My corner of the world isn't small."

Dead silence met his claim. Then Pretorius exploded. "That's all you have to say?"

"No, I have quite a bit to say, starting with certain guarantees you made regarding the Pretorius Program. Your program was supposed to choose women receptive to the idea of marriage."

"My program did choose receptive women. You were supposed to show some patience, remember? You're just like Justice. You can't just date for a couple days, or even a couple of weeks and then pop the question."

"Why not?" Lucius spared a glance toward the door to his office, which Angie guarded with such skill and dedication. He couldn't imagine a better employee. She'd become a vital part of his organization and he didn't want to consider the possibility of ever losing her. "Your program helped me choose the perfect PA within that time frame. And Ms. Colter has proven to be an excellent employee."

"We aren't talking about an employee." Frustration bled through the line. "We're talking about a wife. The parameters for a wife are far more complicated than for an employee. In addition to personality issues and general likes and dislikes there's physical and emotional compatibility. I need to assess each woman carefully and make sure that marriage to you and caring for an infant mesh with her long-term goals and desires. Otherwise you'll find yourself dealing with an unhappy marriage, followed by a messy divorce."

"I told you I don't want any emotional involvement. I want a woman who will function in the capacity of wife and mother the exact same way Angie functions in the capacity of my PA."

"Come on, Lucius. You're being unreasonable and you know it. Why would any woman want such a cold, sterile marriage?"

Because he was cold and sterile. Because at the ripe age of twenty his father had died, and he'd allowed his desire for vengeance to rule his life. Because he didn't trust. Was constantly watching for the next betrayal. How could you build a relationship when you refused to allow anyone in? When opening yourself up to someone guaranteed a wealth of pain?

Other than his father, Lucius had fully opened himself to one other person in his life. A brother in spirit, if not by blood. Geoff. And when Lisa had come between them, she'd destroyed what they'd once shared, utterly and finally. Had shut a door he now realized had been a vital part of his life. Now he stood adrift, a lonely rock in the middle of a tempestuous sea, solid in only one regard.

He would never trust again.

"Listen to me, Pretorius.... Why my future bride would accept a cold, sterile marriage is your problem, not mine. To be frank, I don't give a damn so long as she's a loving mother to Mikey and can create an efficiently run, beautifully appointed home. Someone who is comfortable entertaining clients. Now, I've submitted my order. You assured me you could fill it. So, fill it."

Pretorius blew out a sigh. "Okay, fine. Give me a week to tweak the parameters some more. Then I'll send you a new list. But I have to tell you... We're running out of eligible women in the Seattle area."

Okay, a negotiation. He knew everything there was to know about negotiating. "Then expand the search to the Northwest section of the country. Hell, open it up to the entire United States if it means I'll have a wife within the next three months. You do that, I'll throw in a nice, juicy bonus."

"I may have to pull my assistant in on the project," Pretorius said cautiously. "Do you have a problem with that?"

"Is he discreet?"

There was a long pause, then, "She can be bribed."

"Fine. Then do it."

"I'll be in touch as soon as possible."

"With a list of women that includes my future wife."

Pretorius groaned. "Fine, fine. She'll be on there."

The instant Lucius disconnected the call, he crossed to the bank of windows overlooking a gray and rainy Seattle cityscape. It perfectly matched his mood. He planted his fists on his hips and lowered his head like a bull prepared to charge. Wanting to charge. Wanting to fight free of his current predicament.

How could Geoff do this to him? How dare he go and get himself killed, leaving Lucius with his and Lisa's son. He didn't want to be a guardian to the boy. How the hell was he supposed to raise him, turn him into the sort of man Geoff would have been proud to call his son, when it was so far beyond Lucius's abilities? What had Geoff been thinking?

He picked up his glass of scotch and drank the last of it. He didn't have the heart to be a father. Didn't have the soul for the job. Couldn't imagine years of playing the role of Dad to Mikey, despite having had the kindest, most loving father himself. The sort of father Mikey deserved. The sort of father Geoff would have been. It was so far beyond his scope and ability, he might as well have been asked to catch the moon in a butterfly net.

Damn it to hell! He swung around and heaved the glass across the room. The glass exploded, shattering against the wall, the dregs of scotch and ice raining down the wall like tears from heaven. So he would cheat. He'd hire someone—a wife—to take on his responsibilities. And he'd make her life so safe and secure and plush, she'd never leave him. Even though he couldn't offer her everything a husband should, he could offer enough. A beautiful, richly appointed home. A man who could give her pleasure in the bedroom, even if he couldn't give her love. A life filled with luxury, her every desire fulfilled, her every wish granted. It would be enough, wouldn't it?

He glanced toward the door. Well, it would be enough for most women. Maybe not for his intrepid PA since her every wish and desire revolved around her excelling at her job. Now that he could understand. Understand and admire. Just thinking about her helped him gather himself. Relax. Realize that on this front, he was in control of his own destiny.

Thank God for Angie.

Two

"Not many women can wear that dress and get away with it," Trinity commented. "It's because you're so slender."

Angie tugged at the plunging drape of the bodice. "No, it's because I'm built like a prepubescent boy."

Trinity shook her head. "Honey, that figure is all woman. True, it's not voluptuous, but no one would ever mistake you for a boy. And that shade of aquamarine is stunning on you. It really makes your eyes pop."

After Britt's betrayal, Angie had been reluctant to form a close relationship with another woman. She definitely hadn't been interested in finding another best friend. Trinity had ignored every one of Angie's defensive barricades and steamrollered right over them. It took a full six months before she'd broken through the final one, but once she had, the two became as close as sisters.

Angie gave a quick shimmy. "This dress is too tight. I think I need a size larger."

"It's perfect and you know it. It's exactly what Devlin requested."

It might be exactly what he requested, but it wasn't at all what Angie wanted to give him. Or rather, showcase in front of Gabe Moretti. Maybe if this were a romantic dinner with Lucius, and the dress were meant for his eyes alone… The instant the thought—the dream—popped into her head, she ruthlessly plucked it out again. That would never happen.

She'd heard the gossip about Lisa and her on-again, off-again relationship with first Lucius and then Geoff Ridgeway. The relationship had ended in Lisa's marriage to Geoff two short months after Angie accepted a job at Diablo, Inc.—over a year after her own split with Ryan. Rumors and gossip had flown through the office, hot and heavy, only abating when it became clear that the newlyweds were ecstatically happy. How many times had she driven that point home in an attempt to quell the rumor mill and give her boss some peace? When Lisa announced her pregnancy, and the couple had named Lucius the baby-to-be's godfather, the last, lingering whispers had finally died off.

Even so, Angie saw what no one else did, what Lucius had successfully hidden from all but the most discerning eyes. He was beyond miserable, working day by day to put a stoic face on a hideous situation, which confirmed her suspicion that he'd been madly in love with Lisa. But she knew beyond a shadow of a doubt that he'd never get over losing the love of his life to his best friend, even if Angie couldn't understand why anyone would choose the affable, slightly geeky Geoff Ridgeway over the sexy-as-hell Lucius Devlin.

No doubt losing his soul mate explained his cold-blooded attempts to find a mother for Mikey. He wasn't interested in any sort of emotional involvement; he simply wanted a permanent nanny for the baby—not that it was any of her business.

Angie forced her attention back to the task at hand and turned, frowning at the way the thigh-high skirt clung to her backside, the horizontal pleats giving the illusion of attractively rounded hips. The miniscule skirt showcased mile-long legs, while the three-inch heels made them seem even longer.

"Don't you think it's awfully short?" she asked Trinity in concern.

"Not even."

"A bit low cut?" The question carried an unmistakably desperate air.

"You have great collarbones and a pretty chest." Trinity approached, circled. "I say, show it off."

"I'm not sure this is smart."

"Hey, you said Devlin wanted you dressed to distract. Trust me. This'll distract every living, breathing man within a ten-mile radius. Maybe fifty miles. How are you planning to wear your hair?"

"Up."

Trinity planted her hands on her hips and tilted her head to one side, her spiky black hair, slanted green eyes and gorgeous golden-brown skin making her look like a cross between a cat and an elf. "I'm torn. The back is cut on the low side. If you wear your hair down, you lessen the impact of it. But you always wear your hair up." She gathered the length in her hands and lifted it into a loose and careless ponytail, the curls cascading down the center of her spine. "Okay, this might work. Hair has that flirty, windblown look and yet, you can still see plenty of skin."

“A must, I gather,” Angie said drily.

“A definite must,” Trinity agreed. “Go easy on the makeup. Let your body do the talking.”

“My body hasn’t done any talking for three full years.”

Trinity shot a swift glance over her shoulder. “Girl, don’t go admitting that where someone can overhear you. I mean, that’s just sad.”

“But true.”

“Mmm. You go out dressed like this more often and your body wouldn’t just be talking, it would be screaming out the ‘Hallelujah Chorus’ on a nightly basis.”

Angie didn’t dare admit that her body had never screamed the “Hallelujah Chorus.” Hummed a few bars, but that was about as close as she’d come. “What about jewelry?” she asked, deliberately changing the subject.

“Earrings. Dangles. Preferably silver.”

“I think I have something that might work. They’re beaten silver, a cascade of twisted hearts.”

“Oh, the irony.”

Angie grinned. “Not that I’m obsessive, or anything.”

“Hell, no. Why would you be?” She gave Angie a hip nudge. “Come on. Pay for the thing and let’s go have dinner and drinks. We should celebrate your release from the land of the average and banal.”

Stifling her qualms, Angie bought the dress and heels, then threw in some ridiculously expensive undergarments that were little more than scraps of lace held together by elastic threads. *In for a penny...* She found the rest of the evening far more enjoyable than the torture of clothes shopping. Trinity had a flair for distraction. Of course, it didn’t hurt that they split a bottle of wine over an Italian meal.

Several hours later, she sat back, replete. “I should have bought that dress in a size larger,” she confessed ruefully.

Trinity groaned. "Maybe two. It was those bread sticks. They do me in every time."

"Funny. I would have said it was the tiramisu."

"Not a chance. Desserts here don't have calories. The waiter swore it was true. I might be able to give up bread sticks—or at least cut back a little—but don't ask me to give up their tiramisu."

"Fair enough."

"So are you done brooding?"

Angie blinked in surprise. "Was I brooding?"

"He called you office furniture. That's enough to make anyone brood. But I guarantee The Devil won't call you that ever again." Trinity nudged the shopping bags with the toe of her Choos, intense satisfaction sliding through her voice. "Not once he sees you in that dress."

Angie flinched. "Don't." Though she'd never told Trinity how she felt about Lucius, there was no question her friend suspected something. "Nothing will ever happen. Not with him. He's actually thinking about getting married."

Trinity's mouth dropped open. "No way."

"It's a sensible decision. He needs a mother for Mikey."

"And has he found her or is he in the looking phase?"

"Looking."

Trinity's hazel eyes danced with mischief. "Well, then. Maybe that dress will have him looking in a whole new direction."

It was just a joke, Angie told herself for the umpteenth time, smoothly changing the subject. A tantalizing possibility, but utterly impossible. Unrealistic. And considering it as anything else could only lead to one place. Utter heartbreak. She couldn't go there. Not again. And so she chatted and laughed and tucked her heartache away until she could escape home.

The minute she entered her house, she carefully tucked her purchases into the far recesses of her closet where the outfit wouldn't be in a position to taunt her for the next few days. And even though Lucius asked for the receipts, she refused to hand them over. It didn't seem right to have him pay for the dress, not to mention the more intimate pieces she'd bought. Not when she could wear them on more occasions than their business dinner.

Friday came far too soon for Angie's peace of mind. She left work promptly for a change and refused Lucius's offer to pick her up. Easier to take a cab to the waterfront. She arrived at Milano's on the Sound exactly on time. She loved Joe's restaurant, loved the romantic ambience of it, even though tonight was strictly business. The layout of the interior appealed to her on some basic, feminine level, the overall design making clever use of spacing, angles and elegant furnishings. Joe had even created little nooks and oases that gave the diners the illusion that they were the only patrons present.

Andre, the maître d', greeted her by name as he offered to take her wrap. She could only assume he had one of those impressive memories that allowed him to pair names with faces. His gaze swept over her in a discreet manner, but one which managed to convey deep masculine approval. It gave her confidence a boost, something she badly needed considering the two men she'd soon be dealing with.

"Mr. Devlin and Mr. Moretti have already arrived," he informed her in an undertone. "They seem somewhat at odds."

"Already?"

Andre lifted a shoulder in a shrug that clearly said, "Alpha men, what else do you expect?"

She smiled. "Have they been served drinks?"

"Not yet."

"I have it on good authority that they'll be ordering beef this evening. Why don't you have a bottle of Glenrothes brought to the table. If I'm wrong and they order seafood, swap it out for Old Pulteney."

"Of course, Ms. Colter. I'll see to it immediately."

He guided her to an exclusive section reserved for VIPs. While some of the tables allowed couples to sit hip to hip in the deep, cushioned benches facing the windows overlooking Puget Sound, the table Andre showed her to was a simple round. The two men sat across from one another like a pair of combatants. A vacant chair, facing the windows was clearly meant for her. Great. She loved playing Monkey in the Middle.

She didn't know what alerted Lucius to her presence. But she could tell the instant he sensed her, his body stiffening, his gaze swiveling to narrow in on her. The patent disbelief in his gaze when he saw her almost made her laugh—or maybe cry since it told her precisely what he thought of her as a woman. He was quick to conceal his shock. Too late, she wanted to say.

He shoved back his chair and stood, approaching in order to take her hand in his and guide her to the table as though they were a couple, instead of boss/employee. "Gabe, you remember my PA, Angie Colter."

Gabe Moretti was every inch as gorgeous as Lucius, with hair as raven dark. But instead of eyes to match, his were the shade of antique gold, filled with mystery and predatory intent. He stood to greet her, his gaze sharp and appraising. Then he smiled with singular charm and offered her his hand. "It's a pleasure to see you again, Ms. Colter," he said in a voice that made her think of smoke.

"Please, call me Angie, Mr. Moretti."

He inclined his head. "Let's make it Angie and Gabe,

shall we?" Before Lucius had the chance, he pulled out the chair for her, acting the part of the host—and no doubt annoying her boss in the process. "I believe the last time I saw you, you were shopping for a house. How did that turn out?"

Impressed that he'd remembered, she rewarded him with a broad smile. "I closed on a small cottage in Ballard last month. It needs a bit of work, mostly cosmetic, but considering I picked it up for an excellent price, I don't mind in the least."

"Smart. But, then, knowing Devlin, he only hires the best." He shot Lucius a challenging glance. "Perhaps I should steal her from you."

Lucius didn't rise to the bait. "One of the qualities I look for in an employee is loyalty. You're welcome to make Angie an offer. If she accepts, it simply means my assessment of her was mistaken and I'm better off finding a new PA." He turned his black gaze on Angie and his smile smoldered like the smoke from hell. "Have I made a mistake?"

Good Lord, how in the world had she ended up in the middle of this tug-of-war? Instead of answering the question, she gave Andre a discreet nod, relieved beyond measure when he crossed to the table with the bottle of scotch. It proved the perfect distraction. With the ease of long practice, she turned the conversation to the latest financial market news. That successfully navigated them through the pouring of their drinks. Fortunately, the restaurant owner, Joe Milano, appeared just then with a platter of cold shellfish he'd prepared for them, personally.

He offered each man his hand, greeting them by name. He even took Angie's hand, kissing it with a natural ease that charmed. "You are absolutely delectable this evening. Who's going to look at my food when they can look at you?" he teased. "I should hide you away so my dishes can take center stage once again."

"I'm not sure Maddie would approve of that," Angie replied with an answering smile. At the mention of his wife's name, his brown eyes lit up and the expression that came into his face caused a pang of envy. What she wouldn't give to have a man look like that at the mere mention of her name. "Is she still trying to burn down the house?"

Joe chuckled. "Let's just say I keep her well away from the kitchen. And since our daughters all seem to follow in her footsteps—with one delightful exception—they are also banned."

"A future chef in the making?"

"Without question." Joe didn't linger after that. Wishing them *buon appetito,* he returned to the kitchen.

She didn't give either of her dinner companions the chance to cause further trouble. Once their waiter served them choice tidbits of the appetizer, she nudged the conversation ever so gently into the direction of the most recent changes to building inspections and codes, a subject dear to the hearts of both men. That got them through the appetizers, over the hurdle of a visit from the sommelier and a prolonged discussion of dinner options, before leaping directly into a terse debate over which dish was Joe's most impressive specialty.

Honestly, men never failed to exasperate her.

The instant their dinner arrived, she deliberately turned the conversation to the Richter project, hoping against hope it would get the focus off her and onto business where it belonged. "Your remodel of the Diamondt building was stunning," she informed Gabe with utter sincerity. "Are you planning something similar for this venture?"

"To be honest, I mainly handle the structural renovations." The instant he nudged his empty plate to one side, a busboy whisked it away.

"Who orchestrated the interior design? They did an impressive job of melding a forties retro feel with all the modern conveniences."

Gabe hesitated, his eyes darkening in a way that warned of some deep-seated displeasure. "I hired a San Francisco firm for the remodel. Romano Restorations."

"I'm not familiar with them."

"No, they're a fairly new firm." He glanced at Lucius. "Assuming we can come to terms, we may want to consider them for this job, too."

Lucius tilted his head to one side, his gaze shrewd. "You have reservations," he stated, picking up on the same hesitation Angie had.

"Nothing to do with their work or their owner. Constantine Romano is outstanding at his job. It's his wife who concerns me." He gave a careless shrug, drawing attention to the impressive width of his shoulders and chest. "It's a personal matter, one that has no bearing on business."

A cynical light flickered to life in Lucius's eyes and Angie could guess what he was thinking. "It's not that," she told him before she stopped to think.

Instantly, two sets of masculine eyes swiveled to dissect her. "It's not...what?" they both demanded, almost in unison, and she winced.

She sat for a split second and stewed. When would she learn to keep her big mouth shut? Granted, Lucius had included her tonight because she tended to be good at assessing people and situations. She had a knack for reading between the lines and, for the most part, coming up with accurate conclusions. Still, he probably would have preferred to have that assessment made in private. Oh, well. Too late now.

Taking a moment longer to consider how to answer their question, she went with the truth. The two businessmen were far too sharp to believe anything less. She glanced at Lucius and fought to maintain her equilibrium beneath his narrow-eyed glare. "When Gabe says it's personal, you assumed it meant he'd had an affair with Romano's wife. It's something else." She took a sip of wine in the hopes of settling her nerves. It didn't work. "Something clearly private."

"How do you know?" Again in unison.

She sighed. Could the two *be* any more like peas in a pod? She turned to Pea #1, aka…her boss. "Because he's angry, but not in a you-done-me-wrong sort of way. Plus, his anger isn't directed at both of them the way it would be if he'd had his woman stolen from him." And wouldn't that comment cut close to the bone with Lucius, considering he'd lost his woman to his best friend. She hastened to turn to Pea #2, aka…her boss's occasional competitor. "Considering the temperature just bottomed out to subarctic—shiver, shiver—it's clearly a private matter that you wouldn't talk about regardless of the incentive." She smiled brightly. "More scotch, or should we get down to serious business over dessert?"

"Dessert and serious business," Gabe decided.

"With a little more scotch," Lucius added blandly.

Unfortunately, the going continued to be as turbulent as the chop of the Sound outside the restaurant window, mainly because throughout their discussion, Gabe initiated a mild flirtation with her. His hand brushed hers when he made a point. His fingers lingering on her shoulder whenever he asked a question. He even caught a springy curl and gave it a tug during some teasing remark.

Normally, she'd have flirted right back, fully aware Gabe wasn't being the least serious. But one look at Lucius's expression warned her to play it very, very cool. It didn't make the least sense to her. Hadn't he requested she flirt with Moretti? Wasn't the goal to keep him distracted and off his game? Based on the dark looks she was receiving, the goal had changed without warning. Even worse, the only person distracted was Lucius.

By the time the last bite of a vanilla bean crème brûlée had been consumed, Angie hung from the end of her rope by a tattered thread. Gabe had somehow wrung more concessions out of her boss than she thought possible, a fact that left him smoldering dangerously. That fire threatened to burst to life when Gabe leaned in to kiss her farewell in what would have been an innocuous gesture if he hadn't taken one look at Lucius and then shifted the aim of his kiss, and slowed it, so it caressed the side of her mouth.

Angie decided it might be in her best interest to make a hasty retreat to the ladies' room while Andre ordered her a cab. With luck the two men would have already departed by the time she returned. She was half-right. Gabe was nowhere to be seen, but Lucius remained. He draped her wrap around her the instant she joined him.

She glanced toward the maître d'. "Has Andre ordered my cab?"

"*Our* cab," he corrected. "And yes, he has."

Well, damn. That's what she got for counting the minutes until she could let down her guard and relax. Cursing her luck, she piled a full thirty back onto her tally. "Isn't it out of the way for you?"

"I don't mind. Besides, I'm curious to see the house you bought."

Great. Just great. "No problem," she murmured. Big problem. *Huge* problem. And one she didn't have a hope in hell of avoiding.

"I appreciate your coming tonight," he surprised her by adding. "Ah, here's the cab now."

She followed him from the restaurant into the night air, snuggling deeper into her wrap. The scent of salt and fish flavored the breeze along the waterfront. From the direction of Puget Sound whitecaps foamed beneath a sliver of moon and ferries plied the restless chop, their lights glittering against the blackened sea. The cityscape loomed overhead, glowing with life and vitality. Lucius held the door of the cab and she slid in, praying her skirt didn't ride any higher. To her relief it stayed put, preserving her modesty. She heard Lucius give the driver the directions before joining her. Leave it to him to have every obscure detail at his fingertips, though it gave Angie an unsettled feeling, knowing that Lucius knew where she lived and could relay the address off the top of his head.

Maybe it had something to do with the thick blanket of darkness combined with the lateness of the hour, but his presence filled the back of the vehicle. Every so often a streetlight would pierce the shadows and play across hard, masculine angles. But that only served to emphasize the darkness of his eyes and make him appear tougher, more unapproachable. Like Bogey in one of his film noirs.

She searched for something to say, desperate to break the silence. Not that it was totally silent. Outside the city lived and breathed, filled with noise and lights and movement. But for some reason, it seemed distant and remote from within the confines of the cab, where his quiet breathing thundered in her ears and a visceral awareness grew with each passing moment. She peered into the night, assessing their distance from home. Still too far.

Way too far.

"I'm sorry the evening didn't work out quite as planned," she offered, desperate to break the silence.

"That wasn't your fault." His voice issued from the darkness. Quiet, yet carrying an edge that teased along her nerves, making her painfully aware of her scanty dress—and even scantier self-control. "It was mine."

"I didn't expect him to flirt with me," she confessed. "I thought that was my job."

"Yes, that took me by surprise, too." His head turned. All but his eyes remained in shadow, darkness buried within darkness. But those eyes… Heaven help her, they pierced through the night and arrowed straight into her soul. Could he see her thoughts, sense what she felt? The rational part of her knew it wasn't possible. The more visceral, feminine parts responded to the sheer maleness of him…and wanted. "If you'll recall, I did mention that you're a very attractive woman."

"With the right clothes and hairstyle, that is."

She could feel the burn of his gaze sweep over her. Strip her. "And I was right. That's one hell of a dress, Colter. What there is of it."

Her grip tightened on her wrap and she refused to look at him, afraid to look in case she lost the tenuous hold she maintained on her self-control. What would he do if she fisted her hands in that black silk jacket and yanked him to her? Kissed him in a way no employee had any business kissing her boss? Would he take her? Or reject her?

"You disapprove of my choice?" she asked.

The power of his gaze grew weightier, sharper. So tightly focused she could feel it laser into her very bones. "Hell, no. Though now that I've seen you in this, I'm not sure I can stand having you wear any more of those chair upholstery suits you favor."

"That isn't your decision." Her head swiveled in his direction and she fought to keep her voice cold and distant. "Nor do you have any say in the matter."

"And if I insist on having a say? If I claim the way you dress reflects on me? On Diablo?"

Furious words rose up, fighting for escape, trembling on the verge of utterance. To her profound relief, the cab pulled to a stop in front of her house. Not waiting for Lucius to play the part of the gentleman, she erupted from the cab. "Thank you for escorting me home. I'll see you Monday morning."

She slammed the door closed before he had a chance to reply and flew up the steps of her 1940s era Craftsman cottage. She fumbled in her envelope purse for her key, found it and was just about to jam it into the lock when she heard the slow, deliberate footsteps climbing the stairs behind her. She spun around. The cab was gone.

Lucius wasn't.

"Well?" he asked. "Aren't you going to invite me in?"

Bad idea. Very bad idea. "Sure." *Idiot.* "Would you like a cup of coffee?"

"Sounds perfect."

She fought to address him with a casual air and came within waving distance. Not that she fooled him. Lucius wasn't a man to fool, or a man to make a fool of. He continued to regard her with a watchful gaze, seeing far too much for her peace of mind. "I'll give you the grand tour while it's brewing. Not that it's all that grand," she chattered. It took four tries to get her key into the lock and the door opened. She threw a brilliant smile over her shoulder. "I guess the first improvement on my list is better lighting so I can see to open the door."

He returned her smile, though his eyes were knowing. Of course they were, damn him. Devlin never missed a thing. He stepped across the threshold and closed the door behind him, overpowering the dainty, feminine foyer with an excess of testosterone. He glanced around, nodding in approval. "This is charming, Angie."

"It needs paint. Carpets. Upgraded plumbing." *Babbling!* "But the electrical is sound, as is the basic structure."

He took his time looking around. "I like that the place has its original molding and hardwood floors. So many of the older homes have had those things stripped out and sold to restoration companies."

She led the way to the kitchen and started the coffee brewing. "Speaking of restoration, I was thinking about restoring the '40s look of the place, sort of like what Moretti did with the Diamondt building. Retro appliances. Antiques from that time period." She removed cups and saucers from the cupboard, her enthusiasm taking over. "It has two bedrooms and baths on this level, along with a powder room. One of the baths would be perfect for a claw-foot tub and one of those elegant pedestal sinks. Then there's the upstairs. It's unfinished right now and I'm not sure whether I want to put in a master suite up there or an office."

"A master suite would add more to the resell value. You can always turn one of the downstairs bedrooms into a home office."

She poured the coffee and turned to hand him a cup. He was so close she almost dumped it on him. "Sorry," she murmured, taking a swift step backward that jammed her up against the counter. For some reason she had difficulty meeting his gaze. "There are times I think this place is built more like a dollhouse than a house meant for adults."

"You're nervous. That's a first for you." He tilted his head to one side, his eyes as black as the bowels of hell. "Why is that, Angie?"

She made a helpless shrug. "You're my boss. And we're in my home."

"And we're blurring the lines?"

"Something like that," she admitted. Honesty forced her to confess, "Okay, totally that."

"Normally, we aren't the sort of people who blur lines."

"No."

But she wished she were. If she weren't afraid it would mean losing her job, she'd accept the offer she could read in his gaze. Part of her urged her to do just that. After all, what did it matter? He'd made it clear he intended to marry. If he did, she'd quit. Why not take a chance before that happened? Why not show him that she was so much more than a piece of office furniture. That she was a woman with a woman's emotions. All it would take was a kiss. A single kiss.

As soon as the thought came to her, she instantly dismissed it. Just where would that kiss lead? Straight to bed. To bed, where she'd be able to prove to him beyond a shadow of a doubt that while she excelled as his PA, she was a total disaster as the sort of woman who usually graced his bed. The stunning Lisa had managed to keep two brilliant and powerful men hooked. Angie closed her eyes. She hadn't even been able to hook one.

"Lucius—"

He lifted a hand, cut her off. "Tonight was a disaster. You realize that, don't you?"

Her brows pulled together in consternation. "You said it wasn't my fault."

"I lied. It was your fault."

"Wait a minute. Wait just one damn minute." She set her cup and saucer on the counter, the porcelain singing in protest. "You told me to flirt with him."

"I told you to distract him. You didn't distract him." It

only took a single step in her direction to have him invading her personal space. "You distracted me. And he bloody well knew it. Knew it and took advantage of that fact."

"And you blame me for that?" she demanded indignantly.

"I blame it on that damn dress." Burning flames of desire flared to life in his gaze, sweeping like wildfire across her skin, scorching in its intensity. All she could do was stare in return, bathing in the irresistible flames. "Maybe it would help if you took it off..."

Three

Lucius heard the swift, panicked catch of Angie's breath. God help him. Even that was sexy as hell. Why had he never noticed? How could he have been so blind?

"Have you lost your mind?" she demanded.

"Probably," he admitted. Definitely.

"You can't seriously expect me to strip down—"

"Expect? No. Hope?" He invaded the final few inches between them and caught the flutter of her pulse at the base of her throat, heard the swift give-and-take of her breath. "Oh, yeah."

"I work for you. And this doesn't just blur the lines. It steps way over them."

He reached for her, hooked one of the curls that had taunted him all evening and allowed it to twine around his finger. It clung to him, silken soft and utterly female. He'd watched Moretti do just that and it had taken every ounce of his self-possession not to deck the bastard. Lucius shook his head in an attempt to clear it. He didn't understand what was happening to him, couldn't make any sense out of the strength of his reaction. Angie had worked for him over the past eighteen months and not once in all that time had he ever felt the urge to connect with her on a personal level. To take her into his arms and discover whether that sexy, impudent mouth tasted as good as it looked.

Okay, once.

Nearly a year after he'd hired her, they'd been slogging through the day. It had been an unusually rough one despite the fact that Seattle sparkled beneath a crystalline sky while Mt. Rainier loomed in the distance, putting its stamp of approval on this brief slice of perfection. The September air contained the cool and crisp hint of autumn's cusp, filled with the tantalizing whispers of approaching apple and beer festivals.

But for Lucius, the day would have been better drowned beneath a torrent of wintry rain, slashing the windows at his back and driving an early darkness into his office. Lisa had just given birth to Geoff's son and the ecstatic father had raved endlessly about his newborn son and exhausted, valiant wife. Lucius sat quietly, striving to appear both excited for his best friend and interested in details he'd have just as soon known nothing about. Geoff must have talked for hours before Lucius finally sent him on his way, insisting he take the next couple of weeks off to be with his new family. And all the while guilt rode him, lashing him. He hadn't given his friend the time off out of generosity. Hell, no. He'd done it for himself, selfish bastard that he was.

He hadn't wanted to hear another word about how happy Geoff and Lisa were. Or the minute by minute, second by second details of her pregnancy and childbirth. Lisa had been wrong about one thing. It hadn't taken fifty years of wedded bliss to make him choke on their apparent happiness, but only a short nine months.

The instant Geoff left, delirious at his good fortune, Angie slipped into the room. One look at his face sent her straight to the wet bar where she poured him a stiff drink. Whether she'd heard about his involvement with Lisa through the office grapevine, or used her own deductive skills to reason it out during that first year of her employment, it was clear she knew. Knew, and set out to focus his attention on anything and everything other than Geoff and Lisa.

They worked long into the night, ordering takeout before digging into his latest rehab project. When he finally surfaced, he discovered Angie sacked out on the couch of his sitting area on the far side of his office. As always, she wore one of her godawful suits, this one in a muddy brown. At some point she'd stripped away her jacket, the simple taupe silk shell beneath escaping her waistband and draping across the sweetly subtle curves of her breasts. The skirt had rucked upward, showcasing a gorgeous set of mile-high legs. And the hair that she always pulled away from her face in a tidy knot had loosened, spilling down her shoulders in streaks of bronze and chestnut and a pale sandy brown.

For the first time, he saw Angie as a woman.

He must have made some sound. Or perhaps the undiluted concentration of his gaze alerted her on some primal level. Her lashes fluttered and she opened her eyes, the brilliant aquamarine muted with sleep, darker and more intense than normal.

Until now, Angie had always been one of the most professional women he'd ever known. He could create an endless list of her virtues—all perfect for a top-notch PA— and probably never hit all of her many attributes. But for the first time, he saw the woman behind the employee, a woman who possessed a softness and vulnerability he'd never noticed before. Her breathing sharpened, the semi-transparent flow of silk sliding and caressing her breasts with each rise and fall. For endless seconds they simply stared at each other, while a sharp, visceral awareness tugged at his gut.

Everything within him, everything that made him both a man and a predator, urged him to act. To take. To conquer. To possess. And all the while the thin veneer of civilized behavior, of propriety, kept him frozen in his chair, wanting without responding. Instinct warred with rationality. Teetered. If he went to her, pulled her into his arms, she wouldn't resist. Somehow he knew it with the sort of absolute certainty he'd perfected over his years as a businessman, his ability to assess any given situation with split-second certainty honed to a dagger's edge.

"Lucius?" His name, in a hesitant, hauntingly feminine whisper, slipped across the darkened room. Eve's call to Adam.

He clenched his teeth. "Go home. You're exhausted."

She continued to stare at him with eyes of want and he could practically see the apple cupped in her hands. "What about the prospectus?"

"It'll be here in the morning." He stood, snatched up her suit jacket and tossed it to her. "I think this is the first time I've ever seen the impeccable Ms. Colter wrinkled and out of sorts."

As he'd hoped, the comment snapped her to attention. Catching the jacket midair, she erupted from the couch with a gasp of dismay. If hunger for a fast, juicy bite of that apple weren't still dogging him, he'd have found the way she yanked her skirt into position, tucked in her blouse and jammed her arms into her jacket downright amusing. Trembling fingers attempted to shove buttons through holes. The fact that they were the wrong buttons in the wrong holes only added to her appealing vulnerability. Thrusting her hair out of her face, that long tumble of autumn browns, she made a beeline for the door, turning at the last minute.

She cloaked herself in painful dignity, but it was far too late. He'd seen what she buried beneath. Seen. Been tempted. Hungered. The serpent had invaded Eden and left its mark. "I'll see you tomorrow morning at the usual time."

"No, you won't."

He'd rattled her and he couldn't help taking pleasure in it. "I'm sorry?" she asked uncertainly.

"I'm meeting with Dolchester, remember? I won't be in until after lunch."

"Of course. I'll…I'll just leave now."

He nodded, allowing the apple to roll away, untasted. "Good night, Angie."

"Good night, Lucius," she murmured.

The initial spark of desire he felt then didn't come close to the roar of need cascading through him now. He didn't just want a taste of the apple, he wanted to consume every last, juicy bite in great ravenous gulps. His body continued to hold hers trapped against the kitchen counter and she gave a slight shimmying twist that threatened to drive him insane.

"Don't," he warned. "By all that's holy, don't."

She stilled, the cadence of her breath soft and desperate. He should let her go. He should leave. He should walk away now before they did something they'd both regret. But he couldn't walk away any more than he could stop his heart from beating.

"Lucius…"

He teetered on the brink, the foundation of his control crumbling around him while his name on her lips hovered between them like a siren's song. And then he inhaled it, inhaled her, his mouth coming down on hers while their breath became one, hers one of sweetness, his one of need. She tasted of wine and exotic flavors, her lips like velvet. Her body pressed against his in the most delicious of abrasions, lithe and slender, yet with a delicate, utterly feminine ripeness. He couldn't get enough. She invaded his senses, an intoxicating palette of scent and taste, touch and sound, and all he could think about was drinking her in, sip by sip, until he'd consumed every last drop.

"Don't hold back," he murmured against her mouth. "Let go. Show me who you've been hiding beneath those buttoned-up suits."

She laughed, the sound almost painful. "More buttons. Endless buttons."

He caught her lower lip in his teeth and tugged ever so gently, pleased with the shudder and moan it elicited. "Fortunately for you, I know all about the art of unbuttoning."

"I…" She hesitated, on the verge of telling him something, something important. But then she shook her head. "I can't do this, Lucius."

"You don't have to do anything. I'll take care of everything."

"You don't understand. I don't do this. I *can't* do this," she repeated, this time with an almost desperate edge.

He stilled. "Is there someone else?"

The question escaped with a masculine aggression he hadn't intended, though he knew the cause. Damn Lisa to hell and back for her duplicity, for destroying the one relationship he valued above all others—his friendship with Geoff. She'd left a scar when she'd cheated on him, cheated on him *and* Geoff. A festering wound, one he didn't think would ever heal.

If Angie had a man in her life—news to him—this would end here and now. Lucius refused to put another man through what he'd experienced at Lisa's hands. Nor would he put himself through that sort of pain ever again. His next serious relationship would be perfect—one programmed to order. Pretorius Programmed to order.

His question continued to hover between them, one he could tell she was reluctant to answer. "Tell me, Angie. Is there someone else?"

The question still echoed with aggressive demand. Fortunately, she'd never been intimidated by him, her unwavering directness and honesty an attribute he considered more important than any other in a PA, or a woman for that matter. She managed a laugh, though he could hear the heartbreak edging it and wondered at the cause.

"No, it's not that."

Lucius throttled back, the tension easing away. "Then there's no problem."

Before she could speak the protest forming on the tip of her delectable tongue, he kissed her again. She teetered between uncertainty and surrender, and he could practically feel her objections fading like mist beneath a midday sun. Her arms slid upward along his chest, a delicious caress, while her lean fingers sank deep into his hair, tugging him closer. With the faintest of sighs, her head tipped back in surrender, her lips opening to him. He swept inward without hesitation, diving into a sweetness beyond comparison.

He took his time, savoring everything about her. Her taste. Her scent. The stroke of her hands and the feel of her body brushing against his. His control loosened, fought free of his grasp while sheer, masculine instinct took over. He found the zipper that traced the length of her spine and slid it downward to where it stopped, just above the womanly curve of her buttocks. The dress that had tortured him throughout their evening together parted, gaped and then drifted downward to expose a creamy expanse of skin the texture of velvet.

He groaned. How was it possible that Angie could have hidden such an astonishing wealth of sensual pleasure without his ever suspecting its true extent? He'd been a fool. He eased back just enough to allow the dress to drift away. It caught at her hips, threatening his sanity before gravity stepped in and forced it to puddle at her feet.

She was beyond beautiful, a delicate confection of femininity. Her shoulders were broad and fine-boned, her breasts pert and round, tipped with nipples that made him think of raspberries on cream. Her waist curved gently inward above a boyish flare of hips. But no one could ever mistake her for anything other than a woman, not with such a beautifully rounded backside and legs that seemed to go on forever. The thought of what they'd feel like wrapped around his waist threatened to consume him. How perfectly her bottom would fit in his hands when they joined. When they moved as one. When she came apart for him.

When she was his in the most basic, primal way possible.

She stood before him, a pale blue triangular scrap of silk shyly preserving the final bastion of her modesty, while three-inch heels coyly taunted him. He wanted her. Wanted her more desperately than he'd wanted any other woman—even Lisa.

He hooked his fingers in the elastic at her hips, but before he could strip it away, she took a stumbling step backward, staring at him in open dismay. "Damn it, damn it, damn it." She snatched her dress from the floor and clutched it to her breasts. "You're my boss. We've had too much to drink. And taking this any further is a huge mistake."

He couldn't deny anything she said. It also didn't change how he felt…or what he wanted. "It would be one of the most enjoyable mistakes we've ever made."

"It would change everything and I—" Her voice broke ever so slightly, a poignant, telling little break. "I don't want our relationship to change. I think you should leave and we should forget this ever happened."

He couldn't help but laugh, though the sound contained little humor. "I think it's a little late for that." His gaze wandered over her. "I'm afraid there isn't any way I can forget what you've been hiding under those atrocious suits."

"Try," she snapped. She edged away from him, deeper into the living room. "I'd appreciate it if you'd see yourself out."

He took a step in her direction. Then another. She held her ground for a brief instant, her chin raised to a combative angle. He could see the desire in her eyes and knew she wanted him every bit as badly as he wanted her. Then he saw the heartbreak and the pride, saw the hint of fear and desperation. Oh, not of him. And not of what he might do to her. No, he could guess what caused those particular emotions. He sensed her desperation to fight the sexual urge burning through her and her fear that she'd lose her job if she didn't. Or maybe she'd feel obligated to quit, something he didn't dare risk.

All he knew for certain was it would cost her, seriously cost her, if he took this any further. To his utter shock, a protective urge swept through him, demanding he do whatever it took to shield her from hurt—even if he were the one doing the hurting. Especially if he were doing the hurting. And somehow he knew with a bone-deep certainty it would hurt her if he took this any further. Hell, he should be grateful that one of them had retained an ounce of common sense. For some reason, he didn't feel the least grateful.

"Good night, Angie. Thank you for having dinner with me."

"With you and Gabe Moretti."

That stopped him cold. "You throw gasoline on a smoldering fire, you're asking for it to burst into flames," he warned softly. "Is that what you want?"

She didn't answer. Smart woman. Instead, she turned her back on him and disappeared in the direction of one of the bedrooms. It was a more effective response than anything she could have said. Watching that glorious, nearly naked bottom twitch its way across the room on three-inch heels was a punishment worthy of the devil, himself. Lucius managed a grim smile.

And considering most people considered him Lucifer's kin, he should know.

How could she be so stupid?

Angie huddled within the comforting folds of her voluminous cotton robe and stared unblinkingly at the digital clock while it slowly ticked toward 3:00 a.m. What had she been thinking? Oh, now there was an easy question to answer. She *hadn't* been thinking. She'd been so caught up in her hormonal response to sexy as sin Lucius Devlin, to knowing in her heart of hearts that loving him was utterly hopeless, it eclipsed everything but that single, driving imperative. To have him in her bed and finally know his possession. The temptation of having just a single night with him had proved so overwhelming that she hadn't given a single thought to her precious career—the one thing in her life she valued above all else. Hadn't her mother always warned her to put her career first, that men couldn't be trusted to stick? No doubt the fact that her father had walked out on them when Angie had been a baby was responsible for that particular philosophy. But then hadn't Ryan proved her mother correct?

What would have happened with Lucius if she hadn't stepped back? If she'd allowed him to sweep her along on that mind-blowing tide of lust? He'd have discovered the truth about her, that's what. He'd have discovered she was hopeless in bed. Awkward. Self-conscious. Unable to satisfy a man.

She flinched from the thought. Damn Ryan and the cruel, careless way he'd broken her heart. The way he'd made her doubt herself as a woman. The way she'd cut off pieces of her life because he'd made her believe herself incapable. And damn her for letting him, for giving up on the possibility of having a successful sexual relationship, turning to work as both comfort and affirmation that in this area, if no other, she excelled.

It was ridiculous. She needed to get over it. She needed to find a man—a man other than her boss—who could teach her what she needed to know.

Angie frowned in concentration, the thought taking root, flourishing. It wasn't a bad idea, she slowly decided. If Lucius could entertain the idea of a cold, calculated marriage in order to provide a good home for Mikey, a contract between like-thinking adults, why couldn't she do the same? Oh, not marriage. But a cold, calculated sexual relationship, one designed to teach her the art of lovemaking, the craft of fully exploring her womanhood. It would be no different from when she'd taken classes to teach her the skills necessary to pursue a successful career, a career she now enjoyed to the fullest.

What would it feel like to be as experienced in bed and

in male/female interactions as she was at her job? To fully explore an aspect of her life she'd denied herself in the wake of Ryan's and Britt's betrayal? It would be… Tears filled her eyes. It would be heaven. All she needed was the right man. A man who would be patient and understanding. A man she could trust.

For a brief instant an image of Lucius flashed through her mind before she thrust it ruthlessly away. Don't even go there! Heading down that path offered one thing, and one thing only. Certain and total heartbreak. What she needed was a man who found her attractive and that she wouldn't mind having in her bed. But, who?

Oh, wait. Wait, wait, wait. There *had* been another man who'd shown interest in her tonight.

Gabe Moretti.

A man like Gabe, an experienced man of the world would be the perfect choice. She vaguely recalled there'd been gossip about him at the office. What had they said? Right, right. He was a man who had the reputation for caring about women and who held honor dear. And best of all, he was currently unattached. Add all that together and it made him the perfect candidate to help with her problem.

Angie snuggled into her pillow, her eyes drifting closed. Still, she could dream. She could imagine what it would be like to have Lucius free her from the pain and hurt Ryan and Britt had inflicted. A small smile drifted across her mouth. Too bad she didn't fit his criteria for the perfect wife—whatever that criteria might be. Then she'd have it all. A career she adored. A man more than capable of helping her fully explore her womanhood. And even a baby, one she found utterly adorable. Imagine having the best of all worlds.

It was perfection. Sheer perfection.

* * *

How could he be so stupid?

Lucius stripped down and stepped into the shower, inhaling sharply at the cascade of icy water sheeting over him. At least it helped cool his lust. Somewhat. Though not nearly enough, considering he could still see her, nearly nude and gloriously, perfectly female. He braced his palm against the stone wall and allowed the water to pound down on him, praying it drummed some common sense into his addled brain.

This was Angie Colter, PA extraordinaire, he was thinking about. She wasn't the sort of woman to take to bed on a whim. She was his employee, for God's sake. His responsibility.

Just as Mikey was his responsibility.

"Aw, hell," he muttered. "How could I have forgotten?"

The Pretorius Program. His plan to marry the "perfect" wife and mother. Someone who wouldn't cheat on him. Someone who wouldn't desert him or screw him over. Someone he could trust. Not that he believed he could ever have any of that. In his experience people cheated. Deliberately or otherwise, they screwed each other over. And trust was nothing more than a myth. Trust evaporated like a wispy dream at the first hard bump in the road. And usually that bump had something to do with money.

Isn't that what happened between his father, Angelo "Angel" Devlin, and Angel's best friend and business partner? The death of that trust—not to mention the theft of Angel Enterprises by that partner—had killed his father.

And hadn't it happened again with Lisa? She'd wanted money and had done anything and everything necessary to get it, even marrying someone she didn't love.

Wasn't it about to happen with Geoff's parents, a couple who'd stood like second parents to him. Hadn't they just threatened to file a lawsuit to gain custody of Mikey, claiming Lucius an "unfit" guardian?

He turned off the shower and snagged a towel, relieved that he'd regained a semblance of control and common sense. He was grateful to Angie, grateful that she'd showed such amazing restraint and put an end to a situation that would have caused endless complications on the work front. He'd been a fool to allow lust to interfere with logic. He'd finally found the perfect PA and with one foolish, impulsive act had almost ruined a perfect working environment. First thing Monday morning he'd apologize. Then he'd carefully, gently, politely return them to their former arm's length relationship. No doubt Angie would be relieved.

And then he'd devote more time and attention to finding the perfect wife to match his perfect PA.

He tossed back the covers on his bed and allowed himself to relax against a lake of silk. Punching his pillow into a comfortable mound, he folded his arms behind his head. Still, he could imagine how it would have been. He could imagine having Angie in his bed, as brilliant and amusing and meticulous in the way she made love as she was in the workplace. She'd prove just as trustworthy, too, easing the pain and hurt others had inflicted over the years. A small smile drifted across his mouth. Damn if she didn't fit his criteria for the perfect wife, as well as a PA. It was more than perfect. A multibillion dollar business. A brilliant woman more than a match for him in all the most important aspects of life. And even a mother for Mikey, a baby she found utterly adorable. Imagine having the best of all worlds.

It was perfection. Sheer perfection.

Four

"All buttoned up again, I see."

Angie offered Lucius a cool smile, one she'd practiced endless times over the weekend in order to get it just right. "Same as always."

He didn't say the words, but she could hear them loud and clear: *Not always.*

Just as she'd rehearsed for endless hours to perfect her demeanor and how she intended to act when she returned to work and came face-to-face with Lucius again, she'd also agonized over her clothing. She didn't dare select anything that remotely resembled upholstery. But she also didn't want to wear anything too suggestive. Not that she owned much that could be considered in any way, shape or form the least suggestive. Still, it made choosing the perfect outfit a challenge.

She'd finally settled on a crisp brown suit and café au lait blouse. And though she'd ultimately decided to wear her hair up, it was in a looser style than usual. She looked professional, yet approachable, she decided. The epitome of the perfect PA.

Despite that, Lucius's gaze swept her, stripped her. His eyes glittered darkly, the memory of their embrace lurking there like a menacing shadow. He held her with that single powerful look for a long, tense moment before his mouth curved upward in a knowing smile. "Buttons won't work anymore. I know what you're hiding underneath them."

With that, he disappeared into his office, leaving her with a half-dozen sharp comebacks blistering her tongue, all unspoken. Later, she promised herself. If he made one more comment, she'd cut loose with every single one of them. To Angie's relief, the morning swept toward midday without Lucius making any more suggestive observations. Instead, he filled her schedule to overflowing with a laundry list of endless tasks. Shortly before lunch, she glanced up to see an older couple approaching her desk.

"Hello, Mr. and Mrs. Ridgeway." As always, she was careful to offer them a warm, friendly smile. "Did you have a good weekend with your grandson?"

"Michael was fussy."

As usual it was Benjamin who responded, Geoff's mother cloaking herself in painful silence. Grief continued to hang on the pair, carved deep into their faces and making them appear far older than their early sixties. It had been a rough three months for them, their pain and bitterness deepened by the intense dislike they'd felt toward Geoff's wife, and the blame they heaped on her for their son's premature demise. It didn't make the least sense to Angie, but apparently they felt that the two wouldn't have died if Lisa hadn't insisted on a European vacation as a combination Christmas present and second honeymoon.

For some reason that blame also extended to Lucius

and she couldn't help but wonder if they'd somehow discovered that he'd had a sexual relationship with Lisa, as well—knew and in some emotion-riddled, illogical fashion held him responsible for Geoff's death, too.

"Michael needs a more regular routine," Benjamin continued. "Consistent parenting. Passing him around like a football isn't helping."

To her shock, Tabby Ridgeway spoke up, the first time she'd ever directly addressed Angie. "It won't be for much longer. Our grandson belongs with his own kind, assuming his responsibility for carrying on the Ridgeway line, not raised by a man who puts his career ahead of family, who puts riches before everything else in his life." Her cold gaze reflected the determination sweeping through her voice. "We'll be awarded custody soon enough and then we'll make sure Geoff's son is raised right. Raised to overcome the stigma of having an amoral gold digger for a mother. Raised to resist the temptation his father couldn't."

Angie stiffened and it took every ounce of self-control to answer civilly, though it cost her. Still, she didn't dare say or do anything that risked putting Lucius's guardianship in jeopardy. "I know you're all trying your best under very difficult circumstances. Do you need to see Lucius before you leave?"

Benjamin took over again. "We do need to see him, yes."

"I'll let Lucius know you're here," she offered. "Why don't I take Mikey for you?"

"Keesha hasn't arrived, yet?"

Angie caught the disapproval sliding through the question and deflected it with practiced calm. "It's always a pleasure to spend time with your grandson. I don't mind in the least."

The couple reluctantly allowed her to take the baby,

who reached eagerly for her in clear recognition. The instant she cradled him in her arms, he grinned, grabbing at her finger and tugging it toward his mouth. Who knew she'd be such a natural with babies? Delight filled her. She'd always wanted her own children, longed to experience motherhood. But part of her—the part Ryan had taken such cruel pleasure in giving a good, swift kick—agonized over her own inadequacies. She'd ended up believing that, like in all things domestic, she wasn't capable of adequately parenting a child. Thank goodness the brief amounts of time she'd spent with Mikey had proven otherwise. A fierce determination welled up in her. She would make a great mother, and she wouldn't ever allow anyone to convince her otherwise.

Suddenly aware of the Ridgeways' intense gaze, she glanced at them. "Would you care for coffee or tea?" she asked belatedly, forcing her expression to relax into calm, dispassionate lines.

Before they could respond, the door to Lucius's office opened. He filled the threshold with forbidding power, as dark as the Ridgeways were fair. "Tabby, Benjamin. Good to see you."

It was a lie, Angie knew. In fact, they all knew it, but with the threat of a pending lawsuit, Lucius worked hard to keep their encounters low-key and polite. While he escorted the Ridgeways into his office, Angie indulged her maternal instincts. Mikey was a gorgeous baby and definitely took after his mother—no doubt an unfortunate turn of events from the Ridgeways point of view.

Mikey gazed up at her with huge inky eyes and offered a drooling grin that proudly showed off two pearly-white bottom teeth. He'd worked hard on them this past month and she suspected was working on another, which probably explained his fussiness over the weekend. She crossed to the wet bar and dampened a washcloth she kept on hand. He snatched it from her and stuffed it in his mouth, biting energetically on the cold cotton. She slid a hand down his plump, silken cheek and shook her head.

"Poor little mite. Everyone wants you, though I suspect it's for all the wrong reasons."

For the Ridgeways it was their final connection to their son—a son with whom they'd been estranged following his marriage to the "amoral gold digger" they so despised. For Lucius it was a promise made to his best friend, and a keen sense of honor and duty that demanded he fulfill that promise.

While most would have thought that was the full extent of his feelings toward Mikey, over the past several weeks, Angie had caught a glimpse of something more. Something deeper. Something more powerful. And she couldn't help but wonder if it wasn't because Lucius finally realized that the baby was the embodiment of the two people he loved most in the world, that their spirit continued to live through Mikey. She could only hope so.

The phone rang and she used her headset to answer, leaving her hands free to care for the baby. "Diablo, Inc. Mr. Devlin's office. This is Angie Colter speaking. How may I help you?"

"I thought this was the main man's private line." The voice was female, unquestionably young and brash. And oddly intriguing. "How come you're answering?" she demanded.

"Mr. Devlin is currently in a meeting," Angie explained. "The calls are routed to me whenever he's unavailable to take them."

"Huh. Most hotshot billionaires I know just use voice mail."

The comment gave Angie pause. The caller sounded

more like a teenager than a grown woman. How many hot-shot billionaires did the average teenager know? "I guess you could say I'm Mr. Devlin's voice mail. Beep." Not very professional, but something about the caller brought out the imp in Angie.

Sure enough, the girl chuckled. "Okay, fine. This is Jett. I'm working with Pretorius St. John on a top secret program for your boss man." The information had Angie nudging Jett's age a little higher, though she still sounded more like a teen than twenty-something. "You in the know about it or should I aim for enigmatic?"

Angie hesitated and Mikey chose that moment to smack her with the washcloth. And that's when two bounced against two and exploded into a huge glittering four. Her gaze fastened on Lucius's office door and she replayed that long-ago scene with Ella in her head.

"I don't know how you could possibly think I'd be interested in your insane proposal." And what had Lucius said afterward? She flipped through her memories from that day and keyed in on the one she needed. That he'd proposed to Ella after only knowing her for two weeks. *"I made a business proposition that involved marriage and for some reason that ticked her off. Go figure."* And then a little later Angie had told him, *"I have several calls from a Pretorius St. John. He indicated it was a private matter. Something about a computer program he was personalizing for you."*

She shook her head in disbelief. No. No, it wasn't possible. A *wife?* Was that what the parade of women over the past three months had been about? Why he'd proposed to Ella after just two short weeks? Not even a man as determined and ruthless as The Devil Devlin would implement such an outrageous plan…would he? Angie fought to gather her thoughts into a coherent whole, keenly aware her caller was waiting for her response.

Maybe if she asked a few careful questions, she'd be able to confirm or refute her suspicions. Preferably refute them. "Is this about the program Mr. St. John is fine-tuning for Lucius?" she asked cautiously.

"Yup."

Angie closed her eyes, struggling to control her breathing, struggling even harder to keep her voice level and matter-of-fact. Please be wrong. Please, please be wrong. Because if she wasn't, she couldn't keep her job. Wouldn't. Not if Lucius married. Not when she loved him. She refused to stay in a job where every day would be an exercise in sheer torture.

"This program..." She trailed off, steeling herself to ask the unthinkable. "It's the one to help him find a...a wife?"

"Okay, so you're in the know. Guess you'd have to be, considering that's how he picked you. See, here's the problem—"

"Wait," Angie ordered. This just got more and more bizarre. "Back up. He used this same program to hire a PA? To hire *me?*"

"Well, sure. That's what the Pretorius Program was originally designed for. To help people like Mr. Devlin hire top-notch assistants. Or apprentices. But then when Justice wanted an apprentice/wife, Pretorius tweaked it a bit."

"Apprentice...*wife?*" Was she joking?

"Yeah, it was a bit weird, but it all worked out in the end. Now Uncle P.'s got this side business going. Too busy to find a wife on your own? Let our program find her for you. So we've been on the lookout for a wife for Mr. Devlin for the past three months. Heck, we'd even be happy if we could find him an apprentice/wife." A frustrated sigh issued through the earpiece. "But unlike most of our clients, he's proving sort of tough to satisfy. We've selected tons of women for him, but for some reason none of them are right. Just between us girls, I'm beginning to think it's him. Know what I mean? Every time we turn around he's changing the parameters on us."

Angie's gaze darted to the closed office door again. The murmur of voices from inside continued, unabated. "What, exactly, are his current parameters?"

"Oh, not that much." Deep sarcasm refuted her words. "He wants a mother for Mikey, that's number one on his list. You'd think that would be good enough, right?"

"Right?"

"Wrong, girlfriend." She practically sang the words. "He also wants someone who's a top-notch cook and can entertain both clients and friends on a large scale. You know, throw a five-star party complete with gourmet food and a Vegas-worthy show with only two minutes' warning." Papers rustled and Angie could tell Jett was reading from a form. "He also wants someone classy, who can maintain an elegant home. Not sure if she's supposed to decorate it, too. That's one of my questions. She has to be intelligent. Attractive. And there's other stuff that Pretorius blanked out, which probably has to do with sex."

"Dear God," Angie said faintly. "No wonder he can't find a wife."

Jett snorted. "Ya think? Maybe Justice should just build him a frigging robot instead of driving Uncle P. crazy. I think it'd be easier. Don't suppose you know anyone who fits Mr. Devlin's criteria? Unlikely, I realize, considering I don't think she exists. Maybe in some male-oriented fantasyland, but not in any real world I'm familiar with."

The off-the-cuff question sparked an idea. A crazy, impulsive, totally outrageous idea, so unlike her, the audacity of it threatened to steal her breath away. Not only would it provide Mikey with a mother and potentially assist Lucius if the Ridgeways sued for custody, but it would give her a shot at her own female-oriented fantasyland.

Angie sat there, the possibility dangling before her like a bright, shiny diamond, just begging for her to snatch it up. Why not give it a shot? Why not take the chance? The *risk,* she was quick to correct herself. A very serious risk that could—most likely would—lose her a job she adored. Granted, if it worked out, she and Lucius would both have what they wanted. And if it didn't… Well, she planned to quit her job when he married, anyway, so what did she really have to lose?

"You still there?" Jett demanded.

"Still here. I was thinking… What if I did know someone who would be the perfect wife for Lucius?" she asked.

"Get out. You know someone who can cook, clean, do the party thing and take care of a baby? Seriously? Like a real human woman?"

"Not exactly." She stared down at Mikey and cuddled him closer. "We might have to alter the woman's abilities just a tad."

"Uh-huh." Cynicism replaced excitement. "How much is a tad?"

"Well, totally, since this person can't cook or clean. At least, not on the scale you're suggesting." Yet. "The parties might be on the table. And she flat-out adores Mikey, even if she's a bit inexperienced when it comes to babies."

"Well, thanks for getting my hopes up for nothing," Jett complained. "Who is this person and why would I pick someone so completely wrong?"

Angie took a deep breath. "The person is…well…me. And I don't think I'm wrong at all. In fact, I think I'm the perfect choice."

* * *

Rain beat down on them for the rest of the week in a seemingly unending gray curtain. Friday, the sun made a brave reappearance, battling back the storm clouds, and by late that afternoon gained strength, flowing triumphantly through the window behind Lucius's desk. Streams of soft gold flooded the room and he tilted the printout he held to catch the tidal wave of light. He read the name the computer had kicked out for the umpteenth time.

"How is this possible, Pretorius?" he demanded in disbelief, his hand tightening around his cell phone. "Answer me that. How?"

"I don't know. I'm as stunned as you are."

"You programmed the damn thing. Are you telling me you don't know how your own program works?"

"It must have been the result of this latest tweak in parameters," Pretorius insisted doggedly. "But she's your perfect apprentice/wife."

The name of the "perfect" woman danced across the page in a taunting tango. Angelique Colter, Angelique Colter, his *dammittohell* PA, Angelique "Angie" Colter. "How was her name even picked up by your program?"

"Not sure, but I can guess," Pretorius said cautiously.

"Fine," Lucius snarled. "Guess. But make it an accurate one or I swear I'll reach through my computer and peel your circuits right off your mainframe. Then I'll get really mean. Now explain."

Pretorius erupted into speech. "It's possible that the new program, the program designed to find you the perfect wife, was accidentally connected to the old program, the one designed to find you the perfect PA. Apparently, Ms. Colter is an acceptable candidate for both positions."

"Both."

"Exactly. I guess that makes her more than perfect,

doesn't it?" Pretorius gave a quick laugh, then cleared his throat when Lucius didn't join in. "So the real question is… Would you prefer her for your PA, or for your wife?"

For some reason that one simple question hit Lucius like a towering wave, sweeping his feet out from under him and tumbling him over and over. "I'll get back to you," he said and disconnected the call.

An image of Angie in a tiny triangle of blue blossomed fully formed in his mind. So did the rest of her, a very naked rest of her. He saw her again as he had a week before. Her small, pert breasts—Eve's apples, perfect and perfectly tempting. Those killer legs that went on forever. That long, supple flow of her naked back. That glorious backside, round and biteable. The way that glorious backside twitched when she stalked away from him.

His hand clenched around the printout. Dear God, he could have it all. He could have Angie, probably the most trustworthy woman he knew—not to mention drop-dead gorgeous. He could have a mother for Mikey and, hopefully, an end to the Ridgeway's impending lawsuit. He could have Angie in his bed. A suitable hostess. Angie in his bed. Someone to welcome him after a hard day's work with home-cooked meals. And best of all, Angie in his bed. How perfect would that be? It was every man's secret fantasy. And it could all be his.

He shook his head. Forget the fantasy. He needed to consider more urgent issues than personal gratification, the most important of which was Mikey's welfare. If he believed for one minute the boy would be better off with the Ridgeways, he'd have discussed terminating his guardianship in their favor. Had seriously considered it. But in the three months since the death of Geoff and Lisa he'd had ample opportunity to speak to Mikey's grandparents and watch how they cared for him. And one overriding fact had become painfully clear. They were more concerned about the boy's "tainted" blood and the need to suppress that taint than they were about any other aspect of child-rearing.

Not only that, but they were a cold, hard couple, totally unlike Geoff. Maybe that was why his friend had spent so much time hanging out at the Devlins. Memories of those days gathered around Lucius, as faded gold as the sunlight at his back. A bittersweet smile carved his mouth. His father and Geoff had been as alike as two peas in a pod. Open. Trusting. A friend to all. The irony didn't escape him. Maybe they'd been accidentally switched at birth, he the offspring of the emotionally compromised Ridgeways, Geoff the son of Angel Devlin.

He shook his head. It didn't matter. Not any longer. All that mattered now was Mikey and Lucius's determination to save him from the Ridgeway's tender, loving care—or lack thereof. That left only two questions to consider. First, was Angie an appropriate mother figure for the boy? It didn't take any thought at all. He'd seen how she interacted with Mikey. Seen her light up whenever she held him. Witnessed the ease with which she held him. Fussed over him. How her eyes would track him whenever Keesha was around. She was as maternal as they came. And according to the computer printout, experienced with children.

Which brought him to his second question… How did he convince Angie that she'd rather be his wife than his PA?

He shoved back his chair and paced the length of the office. *Face facts, Devlin.* No one would want to take him on full-time. He was a workaholic. Emotionally compromised. Hard. Ruthless. Not the best attributes in a husband, even a temporary one. So, what did he have to offer a woman like Angie that would induce her to accept the position? Money. That was a given. But from what he could tell, financial gain had never been a driving force in Angie's life. Her career had always been her main focus. So, how did he convince a woman dedicated to her career that marrying him was a better option? There was one lever available to him, though he'd rather not use it.

Angie was crazy about Mikey. If she believed the Ridgeways would win custody of the baby if she didn't agree to his proposition, it might put just enough weight on his side of the scales to convince her to go along with his plan. Well, there was only one way to find out whether he could make an offer Angie wouldn't refuse. Ask her.

He touched a button on his phone and an instant later she appeared in the doorway of his office, electronic tablet in hand. Ever since the night they'd had dinner with Gabe Moretti, she'd subtly changed her appearance. She wore her hair looser, the style more flattering to her delicate features. She'd also changed the type of suits she wore from boxy to tailored. And though she hadn't quite broken loose when it came to the color of the suits, they were far more attractive than they had been.

Of course, ever since that night all he could think about was the earth-shattering kiss they'd shared. The softness of her skin. The perfection of her breasts. The taste of her mouth. And all that could be his. He only needed to convince her that she wanted a different sort of career.

"Come in and close the door," he requested. The minute she'd done so, he crossed to the wet bar and poured her a glass of wine. Her brows shot upward when he exchanged the drink for her electronic tablet.

"Am I going to need this?" she asked uneasily.

"Possibly." He shrugged, setting the tablet aside. "Probably."

Her face paled. "Have I done something wrong?"

He allowed a brief smile to touch his face, despite the seriousness of the situation. "I don't usually offer wine to someone I'm about to fire."

"I'll make a note of it," she murmured. "Or I would if you hadn't taken my tablet."

"You won't need it for this."

She took a tiny sip of wine, probably to fortify herself. "And *this* is…?"

"I have a proposition to offer."

She stilled, an odd expression crossing her face, almost as though she were bracing herself. "A business proposition?"

"In a sense." He poured himself a drink, as well, then gestured her toward the sitting area of his office. He could only hope that this discussion wouldn't end the same way it had with Ella. "Let's discuss it."

Angie gripped the wineglass so tightly it was a wonder it didn't shatter. She knew what was coming and could only pray her expression didn't give her away. Guilt threatened to overwhelm her. Ever since she and Jett had concocted their plan and "accidentally" slipped her profile into Pretorius's ongoing search parameters—with a few vital adjustments—she'd second- and third- and fourth-guessed herself.

Lucius needed a wife. A real wife. One who knew all about babies and running a home and entertaining clients. She didn't qualify at all for the first two of those, and barely scraped by on the third. Angie closed her eyes. But there was one thing the computer couldn't program, that Lucius hadn't thought to add to his precious parameters.

It couldn't program love. Whomever the Pretorius Program chose as Lucius's perfect mate, she wouldn't love him. Nor would she love Mikey, even if she excelled in all those other areas. How could she love a man and a baby she'd never met before? Oh, knowing Lucius, he'd find a capable woman. Tears pricked her eyes. As capable as his PA. But he wouldn't find what he didn't even realize he needed.

Love.

Aware that a tense silence had fallen, Angie opened her eyes to find Lucius staring at her through narrowed black eyes. "I told you I wasn't planning on firing you."

"But…" she prompted softly.

"But I'd like to offer you a different position."

"Within Diablo, Inc.?"

"Not exactly."

She refused to act coy. Not about this. "Is this a position along the lines of what you were offering to Ella?"

She'd caught him by surprise and he took a moment before inclining his head. "You're a smart woman, Angie. One of the many qualities I've always admired about you."

Maybe too smart for her own good. "Tell me what you're offering. And tell me why I'd want to give up the job I currently have—and love—for one that won't advance my career."

"First, the position I'm offering is…" To her surprise a hint of color carved a path across his impressive cheekbones. If circumstances had been different she'd have been amused by it. "Well, I suppose you could call it 'temporary fiancée.'"

"A fiancée," she repeated, tensing. Not what she'd expected. Not at all what she'd expected. "A *temporary* fiancée." What happened to his wanting a wife?

He hesitated. "With so much at stake, I thought it reasonable to employ caution. A trial run makes certain both parties are satisfied with the arrangement. If you'll recall, there was a trial period when I hired you as my PA. It's even more crucial to have one for this position." He blew out a sigh. "God, that sounds so cold and calculated. Sterile."

"Is that what you want?" she dared asked. "Cold, calculated and sterile?"

His eyes fired. "No, of course not. But what *I* want to get out of this arrangement isn't what's important. This is about Mikey."

"Believe it or not, I understand that. I'm not a fool, Lucius. I didn't think you were proposing a real engagement." She fought to remain calm, to ignore that flame building in his gaze. To ignore the nerves clawing at her composure. "What happens if we're both satisfied with the probationary period of our engagement? What then?"

"Then we marry."

It was her turn to hesitate. "Again, other than the honor of becoming your wife and a mother to Mikey—"

"Ouch."

She didn't back down or curb the hint of sarcasm she'd allowed to drift into her comment. Didn't dare. If he ever suspected what she and Jett had done, The Devil Devlin would make her life a living hell. And then he'd get really mean. "Seriously, Lucius. Why would I agree to such an insane arrangement? Why would any intelligent woman?"

"First, I'll pay you far more than what you're currently receiving as my PA."

"Okay, ouch right back at you."

He waved that aside with an impatient air. "Look, I know that money doesn't drive you. But it's a start. Let's discuss what the job entails and then you tell me what you want in the way of compensation."

"Fair enough. What would my duties include?"

"First and foremost, as you've already guessed, I require a mother for Mikey. I'm sure you're aware the Ridgeways are talking about suing for custody. So far, I've convinced them to hold off, but one of their arguments is that I don't have a stable home life. I'm dependent on outsiders for Mikey's care. Having a wife whose primary duty is to raise the baby would go a long way toward appeasing them. You have an excellent rapport with Mikey already and you've been very good with the Ridgeways, something they've both noticed and commented on. And it's obvious that your maternal instincts and your kindness are a genuine part of who you are as a person."

"I'm not sure how kind I've been toward the Ridgeways, but they're Mikey's grandparents and Geoff's parents. They deserve my respect, even if I don't agree with their parenting style," Angie stated simply. "Plus, I flat-out adore Mikey."

Lucius grinned. "Even teething?"

She relaxed enough to return his smile. "Even teething." She gestured for him to continue. "What's next?"

"I currently have a housekeeper who takes care of maintaining the house and providing meals. But she's informed me she plans to retire."

Angie lifted an eyebrow. "You want me to cook and clean as well as care for Mikey? Seriously?"

He frowned. "I understand you're a gourmet chef."

Time for a little honesty. "That's a gross exaggeration. I putter in the kitchen." Boiling water. Throwing together a prepackaged salad. Fixing a decent cup of coffee. "But if you're expecting gourmet meals, you have the wrong woman. You're a billionaire, Lucius. Is there some reason you can't hire a housekeeper to handle the general cooking and cleaning?"

"No, no of course not." She could see him making a swift alteration to his game plan. "What about staging events for entertaining large groups of people?"

She could learn. How different could it be from some of the business events she'd helped plan for Diablo? "Sure."

He relaxed ever so slightly. "And you can oversee the domestic end of things."

"I haven't agreed to anything, yet."

Lucius inclined his head. "True enough."

"So far we have the care for Mikey, the organization of the house and entertaining friends, clients and business associates. What else?"

"One final requirement." He set his drink aside, untouched. "As you're probably aware, I live in the penthouse apartment of this building. My plan has always been to find a house better suited to entertaining. With Mikey's advent, I've moved those plans forward. I recently purchased a home on Lake Washington, but it needs a face-lift. It needs a creative woman with an eye for color and design, who also possesses impeccable taste, to oversee those improvements."

Uh-oh. Angie could see where this was heading. Straight off a cliff and into a vat of hot water. Scalding hot water. What the hell had Jett been thinking to add that particular talent to her curriculum vitae? And why in the world would Lucius buy into it? Or had it not occurred to him that a woman who dressed like chair upholstery might not have the best eye for design and color, let alone impeccable taste?

"Are you insane, Lucius?" she inquired politely. "I mean, seriously. Your little laundry list of requirements is a lovely dream. The perfect male fantasy, no doubt. But that's all it'll ever be. It's the height of arrogance to expect one woman to do all that, especially a woman with an ounce of brains, common sense or self-respect. There isn't one item you've detailed that isn't, on its own, a full-time position. Expecting a single person to handle all of them…?" She shook her head. "That's not going to happen. It's certainly not going to happen with me."

He nodded, almost as though he'd anticipated her objection. "Fine. Let's open negotiations. If we hire a housekeeper to handle the domestic chores—cooking and cleaning—all you'd need to do is delegate and supervise."

"That would be a definite improvement. As for Mikey, you still need a part-time nanny to cover for—" She started to say "me" and smoothly changed gears. "To cover for your fiancée/wife when she's entertaining or meeting with the decorator. Or knowing you, dealing with the slew of additional tasks you'll undoubtedly dump on her."

"Keesha is a temporary full-time hire. She made that clear from the beginning. Apparently, she has a mother who isn't well and needs her assistance. But I've already asked if she'd be available for part-time work and she's agreed. Does that satisfy you?"

Angie inclined her head. Now for the more distasteful part of the arrangement. Though she didn't want to ask about the financial end of their bargain, if she didn't address the issue, he'd suspect something was off. "You mentioned payment. Just out of curiosity, how much are we talking?" He named a figure that made her grateful she was sitting. It took her an instant to gather her wits sufficiently to ask, "And if the job doesn't work out?"

He shrugged. "Then you could return to your position as my PA, with a comfortable bonus for your efforts. No hard feelings on either side."

She simply looked at him. "You know better than that, Lucius. If our relationship falls apart on the personal side of things it would have a serious effect on any future working relationship. What happens if one or the other of us wants to sever all ties? I'd be giving up a job I love, a career that's important to me, and for what? To be your domestic goddess?"

He chuckled, the sound sliding through her like a velvet touch. "Is that what I'm hiring? A domestic goddess?"

"Actually, the job title should be domestic slave." Angie leaned back, relaxing for the first time since the start of their discussion. She took a bracing sip of wine, a cool, refreshing Fumé Blanc. It helped steady her for the next topic of conversation. "There's one part of this job we haven't discussed."

"Which is?"

"Sex."

"Ah." An expression came into his eyes, one that had her throat going dry and a hot pool of want forming in her belly. Waves of it lapped outward, roiling and seething in endless demand. "How could I have neglected something so vital?"

"I gather that's a 'yes.'"

"No."

She stiffened, shocked by his answer. Had she miscalculated? Had she read more into the night they'd had dinner with Gabe Moretti? Had he considered their kiss a mild and forgettable flirtation, easily dismissed, while she'd built it up into something far more serious and memorable?

"Not a yes?" she asked faintly.

"No, not a yes," he responded gravely, "but rather a *hell,* yes."

Her mouth twitched and a laugh escaped before she could control it. Then she realized that it wasn't funny. Not considering her issues. Not considering that she'd planned to approach Gabe Moretti over this very problem. Her laughter died and she regarded him with nervous apprehension.

"What's wrong?" His eyes narrowed. "You must realize that if we're going to become engaged, probably married, that a sexual relationship would be an important part of the equation."

She lifted a shoulder in what she hoped was a casual shrug. "You didn't mention it as one of your conditions, so I can only assume it's not a very important part."

"Allow me to prove otherwise."

Before she could react, he took her hand and gave a quick tug. Unable to resist, she tumbled straight into his arms, straight into his mouth…and straight into heaven.

Five

It took only that one kiss for Angie to confirm that her first embrace with Lucius hadn't been a fluke. That if anything, the explosive desire was more intense, searing them in endless heat. She couldn't get enough, didn't think she'd ever get enough. Not of Lucius. Not of his touch, his unique taste.

His mouth moved on hers, a blatant taking, and she moaned in pleasure. He offered endless possibilities on every front. The chance to be a mother. To be a wife. To form a relationship with the man she loved. And maybe, just maybe, she'd be able to explore the sexual side of her nature without fear of rejection.

Her blouse fell open beneath his busy hands and he cupped her breast, stroking the pad of his thumb across the sensitive tip. She shuddered, helpless beneath the onslaught of sensations. How could she have thought, even for one tiny minute, that she could give herself like this to Gabe Moretti. The mere idea now seemed obscene. It was Lucius she wanted. Lucius she loved.

Lucius who might reject her the way Ryan had.

She stiffened in his arms, fighting her way free of the embrace. Lucius released her without protest, but something in his expression warned that next time he wouldn't show such consideration, let alone restraint. "We need to finish our discussion," she informed him. "Nothing is settled and until it is..." She trailed off, heat washing into her face.

"No sex?"

She turned on him. "You're still my boss, Lucius. If we can't come to terms, that isn't going to change. I can't... We can't..." She spun away, struggling to refasten her bra, fumbling with buttons and buttonholes. Why was it that every time she was with him, she came undone? Literally. "If we make love and you end up with someone else as your fiancée/wife it would be more than awkward and you know it. It would mean I'd have to find another job." Of course, she'd have to do that, anyway, one of the primary nails in the coffin she was busily building.

"Why?"

Was he kidding? She turned, glared. "Don't be an ass, Lucius. You know damn well why. Do you really expect to take me to bed one night and then marry another woman the next?" Apparently Ryan had thought so. "And I'm supposed to be okay with that? Well, news flash, ace. It's not okay with me. And it shouldn't be okay with you."

Something in his reaction acknowledged that her words had impacted harder than she'd anticipated. Temper flared, though she didn't think it was aimed at her. "Angie—"

But she wasn't finished. "You know, I was considering having an affair with Gabe Moretti." She had no idea where the words came from, just that anger drove her toward recklessness. "Maybe I should have a quick fling with him before starting this new job you're offering. I'm sure you wouldn't mind. After all, that wouldn't be the least awkward, would it? You wouldn't want to end all association with him. With me. Would you, Lucius?"

Dead silence followed and she shivered, belatedly closing her mouth. Oh, damn. Slowly, Lucius rose, more intimidating than she'd ever seen him. His eyes burned with hellfire, his expression carved into taut, furious lines. Tension and blatant male aggression poured off him. Unable to help herself, she stumbled backward a step. Her gaze shot toward the door, desperate for escape. But it was far too late for that. Far too late to do anything other than watch him come for her, striding across the room like vengeance incarnate.

"I swear to God, if you go anywhere near Gabe Moretti—"

Cornered, she fought back. "You'll what? Fire me? Why, Lucius? Oh, wait. It couldn't possibly have anything to do with what's happening between us. With how you'd feel if I took another man into my bed when we were in the middle of 'negotiating'—" she encased the word in air quotes "—a sexual relationship. If our negotiation falls apart, what is it to you if I sleep with someone else?"

He swept her comments aside as though they were of little to no consequence. "Why were you considering an affair with him?" he demanded.

"Oh, that is so typical of a man," she stormed at him in response. "Ignore my points because the only thing that matters is marking your territory. Well, I'm not a fire hydrant, Lucius. So, back off."

To her amazement, he did. Just a single step. But at least it gave her a tiny amount of breathing space. "When did you come to this decision?" he asked. "And why?"

"My reasons are private. As to when..." She gave it to him straight, even though the truth would only escalate the situation. "I decided the night you kissed me."

His back teeth snapped together and the muscle along his jaw twitched. "Why?"

"You're my boss. I can't have an affair with my boss."

"He's my competitor."

"On occasion. On rare occasions. Shortly, he'll be a business associate." She struggled to remain calm and poised. "And news flash... He's not *my* competitor. He's not *my* business associate. And most important of all, he's not *my* boss."

"It's a conflict of interest."

"You're grasping at straws. I know how to keep my mouth shut when it comes to business matters. You know it, too, or you'd never have hired me or kept me as your PA these past eighteen months. I would never give Gabe Moretti inside information and you damn well know it."

He spun around and paced the full length of his office before turning to face her again. He'd regained a modicum of his legendary control, though she could still see the fury smoldering just beneath the surface. "Why, Angie? Of all the men in the whole of Seattle, why him?"

A choice loomed before her. She could tell him the truth, humiliate herself in front of a man who was her employer—potentially her fiancé. Or she could refuse to answer and risk losing her current job, as well as the one he was offering—a position she wanted more than she could express. Tears filled her eyes and she blinked them back, refusing to allow them to fall.

But he caught her distress. His anger faded, replaced by bewildered concern. "Hell, Angie, don't cry. I couldn't handle it. Not from you." When she simply shook her head, he approached. “What is it? I’m missing something here, something important. What?”

“It’s personal. Private.”

That gave him pause. She could see his brilliant mind sifting through possibilities. “Something you thought Moretti could help you with?”

She didn’t bother denying it. “Yes.”

“By having an affair?”

Her mouth compressed. “Yes.”

“Why him?” he asked again. Pure masculine frustration ripped through his words and she could hear the real question behind the one he asked. *Why him and not me?*

She chose her words with care. “Because we would both know the score going in. We would both understand that it’s a temporary, mutually satisfactory arrangement. Because there wouldn’t be any hard feelings or emotional fallout afterward.”

Lucius froze and his expression closed over, preventing her from reading his thoughts. He’d always been good at that. No doubt it was part of his success, part of what helped him build a billion-dollar business. “And that’s enough for you? Is that part of your reluctance to accept the position I’m offering? You don’t want anything more than a sexual relationship?”

She couldn’t answer him for fear she’d cry. *No!* It wasn’t what she wanted. Not at all. That’s what she wanted with Gabe, not with Lucius. But how did she explain that? How could she explain to him that she’d fallen in love with him, wanted more than anything to have a long-term personal relationship? She couldn’t. Not without revealing how she truly felt. No way would she give him that sort of power. She didn’t dare.

“I don’t see any purpose in discussing what I want or don’t want from a relationship—specifically, *our* relationship—until we've worked out an agreement," she informed him as calmly as she could manage. "And in case you hadn't noticed, we seem to have gotten off point on some of the terms currently under debate."

He cocked an eyebrow, his mouth taking on a sardonic slant. "I'm impressed, Colter. You've managed to reduce sex to a business addendum." He noted her blush, clearly took grim satisfaction in it. "It's called a kiss. Something I found very much on point considering the nature of the position I'm offering."

Is that all it had been to him? A kiss? How was it possible that one kiss from Lucius Devlin managed to leave her totally undone, while his control remained absolute? It wasn't fair. Even worse, Lucius was a brilliant man. Eventually, he'd cop to how she felt, which made her more determined than ever to hold him at arm's length until they'd hammered out the details.

She lifted her chin and shot him a cool look. "Kissing me isn't on point until we reach an agreement." When he would have argued, she held up her hand. "How many times have you told me that a deal isn't consummated until the contracts are signed, sealed and delivered?"

"And the money transfers hands."

She tried to conceal how much his comment hurt. "You know what I mean."

"No consummating until it's a done deal?" he asked drily.

Relief flooded through her at the reluctant acceptance his question signaled. "Exactly."

He crossed the room and retrieved the drink he'd set aside when they'd started the conversation. It seemed hours ago, yet couldn't have been more than twenty minutes. His gaze remained fixed on her in a manner she'd seen all too often. He was considering the problem from all its various angles. Right now she was an opponent in a business negotiation, which put her at a severe disadvantage. He proved it by approaching like a predator stalking its prey.

"Point One," he began. "Even if you refuse the job offer, I still don't want you seeing Moretti."

"That isn't your decision and you know it." She held up her hand before he could argue. "Stop it, Lucius. You cannot dictate my personal relationships and that's final."

"Yet," he corrected, "that changes the minute I put my ring on your finger."

"Just remember that goes both ways," she shot right back.

The minute he absorbed the comment, he stiffened. "I wouldn't cheat on you."

She didn't respond, simply fixed him with an unflinching gaze.

"Son of a bitch," he said softly. "Are you talking about my affair with Lisa?"

No way was she touching that one. "Not at all. I'm talking about a crucial deal breaker to the job currently under discussion."

He simply shook his head. "Somehow I think we're talking about Lisa. Just in case, let's address it so there aren't any lingering questions." His expression remained empty, still giving nothing away, making it impossible to get a read on him. "Lisa and I had an affair. After it ran its course she turned to my best friend, Geoff. When that relationship didn't work out, when it ended badly, as well, she dropped by my apartment. She claimed her affair with Geoff had been a terrible mistake. I compounded that mistake by giving her a shoulder to cry on. As I'm sure you can guess, one thing led to another. It wasn't planned. It was one night and only one night. In retrospect, it wasn't one of my smarter decisions. In fact, it was damn stupid."

"I wasn't asking." Didn't even want to hear. She got that Lisa was irresistible to men. That she had something that Angie couldn't possess if she lived to be a hundred. That she was the type of woman Lucius wanted, a type Angie would never be. Could never be. And it brought home the brutal fact that he would never love her. She fought to keep her voice level, when all she wanted was to weep. "To be honest, I'd rather not know."

"If we're putting our cards on the table, you deserve to know. Now you do." He lifted an eyebrow. "Any cards you'd care to throw on the pile?"

Oh, God. She struggled to conceal her alarm behind a calm facade. "Not right now, thanks."

"That suggests there are cards."

"We all have cards. Right now, mine remain facedown."

"Fair enough." He gestured to the sitting area. "Are you interested in continuing our negotiation, or should we walk away from the table and resume our former business relationship?"

That wasn't possible, not after their latest kiss. He had to suspect as much. But if she continued with their negotiation it would be with eyes wide open, aware he'd never feel for her what she felt for him. If she couldn't accept that, better she walk away. Now. There existed an outside possibility they could return their working relationship to status quo. Well, almost status quo. This second kiss would make it far more difficult to find their way back to familiar ground. That didn't change her options. Retreat… or gamble everything. Not that there was any real question.

She summoned a cool smile. "I'd like to hear the rest of your offer and see if we can't come to terms. I think we've resolved your first point. Shall we simply agree to a fidelity clause?"

He approached again, invading her personal space, watching her helpless reaction to his proximity. "That would be acceptable."

"What's your next point?" she asked, fighting for equanimity.

He took a long swallow of his drink before setting it aside. Hunger glimmered in the depths of his inky gaze, a clear warning of what his next point would be before he even opened his mouth. "Point Two. Sex."

"Why doesn't that surprise me?" she asked wryly.

"I don't know, since it's surprising the hell out of me." He tugged at one of the loose curls dangling along her neck. "I assume we're also in agreement there? If it makes you feel any better, I'll even agree not to expect anything more from you than a purely physical relationship. Will that satisfy you?"

No! "Yes. That would satisfy me." She wanted to weep at how neatly she'd been boxed in, or rather, out of a personal relationship with Lucius, though she didn't have a single doubt he was delighted by the arrangement. Sex without strings. The perfect fantasy. She stepped away from him, forcing him to release the lock of hair he'd twined around his finger. She resumed her seat in the sitting area, anything to give herself some space from the strength of his personality. She needed to think straight if she were to win any concessions in this devil's bargain. "Assuming the trial period goes well, we'll marry?" she asked.

"Absolutely. Point Three. I don't want too long a trial period." He followed her, also sat. "The Ridgeways are on the verge of suing for custody of Mikey."

She frowned in concern. "It's gotten that contentious?"

His mouth tightened. "I suspect they hired a private investigator who uncovered the fact that I had an affair with Lisa. They informed me they're concerned that between Lisa's bloodline, as they refer to it, and my own questionable judgment, Mikey's welfare is at risk."

"Yes, they said something similar to me," she murmured. "I don't like the sound of that."

Their gazes met in perfect accord. "Nor do I."

"What happens to our arrangement if guardianship is awarded to the Ridgeways?"

"I believe that's Point Four. If I can't get it reversed, our marriage will be dissolved. In addition to your salary, you'll also be suitably compensated for your time and for the interruption to your career." He mentioned an amount that stunned her.

"Don't be ridiculous, Lucius," she protested. "That's… that's obscene."

He chuckled, the sound low and warm and strangely intimate. "It's not obscene. A trifle extravagant, but I suspect you're worth it."

"I'm not sure I like the sound of that."

His brows snapped together. "I'm not paying you for sex, if that's what you're thinking. I'm paying you for precisely what I said. Your time and the hit this job will mean to a career that's a vital part of who you are as a person. The money will allow you to pursue a course of study after the dissolution of our marriage so you can once again enter the workforce with marketable skills. Or you can sit at home and twiddle your thumbs, for all I care. If you invest the funds intelligently, you'll be in a position to choose what you want to do with your life from that point onward, while living quite comfortably for the rest of your life."

She edged away from the topic. "And if you're awarded

permanent custody of Mikey? What happens to our marriage?"

"Fair warning, I fully expect to be awarded custody, which brings us to Point Five. I'll require a guarantee that you'll remain with me for at least six years. Mikey will be of school age by then, which puts him at a less vulnerable age. After that, we can renegotiate terms."

"Very businesslike," she observed. Painfully businesslike. "Very cut and dried."

"Would you prefer me to lie?" A hint of irritation swept through the question. "To wrap everything up in a pretty tissue of fantasy tied together with fancy ribbons of pretense? Will that make our agreement more palatable?"

"No. Of course I don't want that."

She wanted a pretty truth tied together with ribbons of love. But he wasn't offering that and she was an utter fool if she thought that by agreeing to this devil's bargain he might one day come to love her. Determination filled her. But she could try. She would definitely try.

"So, what's left to discuss?" he asked.

She did a swift, mental run-through of their points so far. "Point Six? Is that where we left off?"

"Sounds about right."

"Let's label this one 'My Responsibilities.' I want to clarify what you expect of me," she said and proceeded to tick the points off on her fingers. "I will have the full-time responsibility of Mikey except when family obligations require a part-time nanny." She used the word *family* with deliberation, relieved when he nodded his acceptance. Might as well start the way she intended to proceed. "You'd like me to handle all aspects of entertaining friends or clients, but you agree to my hiring a housekeeper to handle the cooking and cleaning. And you want me to decorate your Lake Washington house. You do realize that I'll also require the assistance of a design firm in order to make the necessary improvements to your home?"

"*Our* home. I have no problem with that."

She warmed at his correction. "And anything we've forgotten to cover we can negotiate during our trial period?"

"Absolutely." He tilted his head to one side. "Do we have an agreement, Ms. Colter?"

She took a quick, steadying breath and took a reckless leap off the proverbial cliff. "We do, Mr. Devlin."

"In that case, there's nothing stopping us from doing this..." She realized his intentions a split second before he repeated the same maneuver he'd used earlier, and yanked her out of her chair and into his arms. "You have no idea how badly I want to see you naked again."

Finally.

Lucius would finally have Angie back in his arms. And in very short order he'd have her naked and in his bed. He could see the shock and protest building in her stunning—and stunned—aquamarine eyes. But he could also see the desire. The delicious memory of their almost tumble shyly peeking around the sensible restraint she normally possessed. About damn time.

"The Ridgeways asked to have Mikey again this weekend because it would have been Geoff's birthday. I felt the most diplomatic option was to agree. Since I'm through with my appointments for the day, we can slip upstairs to my apartment and consummate the deal with no one being the wiser."

"Lucius, I'm not sure—"

He couldn't contain himself another minute. He captured her bottom lip between his teeth and tugged. She rewarded him with a soft, hungry groan, one that instantly had him turning hard as a rock. His tongue flirted with hers, then sank into unbearable sweetness while his fingers plunged into the weighty thickness of her hair. He combed it loose, the silken curls tumbling free around her shoulders. The color never ceased to amaze him, an endless spectrum of browns from tawny to bronze.

Lucius managed to gather Angie up and urge her toward the private elevator that accessed the penthouse suite. The doors opened and they practically fell into the car. He fumbled for his access card, all the while deepening the kiss. He had no idea how he managed. Sheer desperation, no doubt. The instant the doors parted, accessing the penthouse foyer, Lucius swept Angie into his arms and carried her directly toward his bedroom. And then he did what he'd been wanting to do ever since he'd last kissed her.

Piece by piece, he stripped her. First, her suit jacket. Then her skirt. Her blouse was next, allowing him to see her as he'd dreamed endlessly of seeing her. She stood before him in nothing but garter and stockings—color him surprised—and panties and bra, the set a lovely shade of bronze that somehow mated with the streaks running through her hair and made her appear like some sort of bewitching autumnal goddess. Slender as a willow, he could only look…and want. Only, this time he would also possess.

He shrugged off his own jacket, ripped at the tie constricting his neck. She tackled the buttons of his shirt while he unbuckled, unzipped and ripped away clothing with impressive speed. And then time stilled. Late-afternoon sun slipped through the window of his bedroom and splashed across the room to where Angie stood, painting her in muted gold.

Once again he saw it, a painful and utterly feminine vulnerability that went to the very core of her. It brought out his protective instincts, the strength of them catching him by surprise. When had that happened? Why had it happened? What was it about her, a woman far stronger in some regards than Lisa, and yet far more fragile in other ways, that caused the most primal of masculine instincts to well up inside of him? She didn't want that from him. She'd made that perfectly clear. She wanted a sexual relationship and no more.

Well, he could give that to her. He was only too happy to give it to her.

But that didn't change how she affected him, the quiet urge to treat her tenderly, with a passion that transcended a mere sexual encounter. How was that possible? Unable to resist, he reached for a lock of her hair and wound it around his fist, drawing her to him. He inhaled her, drew in her essence and allowed it to brand him inside and out, to mark him in some way that would make her forevermore a part of him.

"How could I have worked with you for a full year and a half and never seen?" he murmured.

How could he not have seen who she was at her very essence? How beautiful she was, when stripped of her camouflage? The sheer force of woman that made her eclipse every other woman he'd ever been with. Made them seem…less. Made them seem shallow and incomplete, a meal that no longer satisfied. How could he not have seen the veils upon veils of her that tempted and taunted and urged him to strip them away, one by one, until he knew her as intimately as she knew herself?

"You're seeing me now," she whispered. "I just don't know if you're seeing the real me."

He nudged her chin upward and kissed her, slowly this time. Gently. She was like the first sip of a rare and delicate wine, an explosion of subtle flavor that blended into an intoxicating whole. "You taste real." He released the clasp of her bra and watched it slide away. "You look real."

She swallowed and he saw a hint of nerves. "Touch me and see if I feel real."

Hardly daring to breathe, he cupped her breast, kissed each tip, watched as the nipples tightened and pearled for him. "Oh, you feel real. Very real."

He crouched in front of her, taking his time to release her stockings and slide them down endlessly long, lean legs. They were gorgeous legs, fine-boned and supple, with strong, sweeping lines. He traced the silken length with his fingertips, from narrow ankle to inner thigh. She shuddered beneath the stroke and he heard the breathless moan explode from her. It only took a moment to unfasten the garter and discard it, leaving one final barrier between them.

Instead of a blue triangle like before, this one was bronze, just a tissue-thin silk and lace bastion of modesty, begging to be breached. He pressed his mouth to the center, inhaling her, warmed by her, drinking in the perfume of her desire. Gentle, gentle, gentle, he eased the elastic from her hips and bared her. Wanted her. Needed her. Would do anything to have her.

And then he ravished her, sending her over before she could draw breath to cry out. Her back bowed in reaction at the same instant her knees buckled and he tipped her backward as she flew apart, so the silk duvet cushioned her fall. He stood for a moment, looking his fill at the woman he intended to make his.

Her lashes fluttered against her cheeks and then she lifted her gaze so it clashed with his. He didn't think he'd ever seen anything more glorious than those eyes, drenched in wary shadow and a painful want. They overwhelmed a face edged with elegance and a classic, ageless beauty. Understated, like her delicate bone structure and graceful feminine curves, a shimmer of pale light against the darkness of the duvet. She was a flawless diamond of incalculable value, eclipsed by gemstones who appeared larger and flashier, but were infinitely less precious.

And she was his.

He took her mouth in a nibbling bite. Sank inward. He couldn't get enough of her, didn't think he'd ever get enough. Angie shifted beneath him, her arms stroking upward along his arms, then cupping his face.

"Lucius..."

Just his name, that one word a whisper that slipped from deep inside her to deep inside him. Her fingers slid into his hair, anchoring him, and she lifted her leg, gliding it along the length of his own leg. He shuddered beneath the slow, relentless stroke. She bewitched him. Stole sense and sensibility. All he wanted was to lose himself in her, to make her his in every sense of the word. But a small alarm sounded in the back of his head, growing progressively louder with each moment that passed, until the reason finally penetrated.

"Protection." The word escaped between kisses. "Give me a minute..."

"Hurry." The word was both demand and plea. "Please, hurry."

Lucius reached to one side, fumbled in the drawer of the bedside nightstand. Groped for the packet. Swore when it took three tries. Swore again when it defied his attempts to open. She dared to laugh, scooping the wrapper from his hands and somehow getting it open. And then her cool, skillful hands were on him, rolling along the length of him as she sheathed him, threatening both sanity and control.

"Better?" Angie asked.

"Hell, no." He palmed her lovely bottom and settled between her parted legs. In one swift stroke he mated them, a joining of such utter perfection it took him a moment to speak. "There, that's better. Infinitely better. Unimaginably better."

With a sigh of pure pleasure, she gathered him up, wrapping those endless legs around him and twining her arms tight, tight, tight. And then she moved with him, revealing a charm and style he'd never experienced with another, blending male and female in a dance of perfect synchronicity. *Mated. Branded. Joined.* The words became new to him, the definition honed to a meaning that would forevermore include her at its heart. And through that mating, that branding, that joining, he absorbed her. She became part of him, melded into the very fiber of his being.

Lucius didn't know if she understood what had happened, this claiming. Couldn't do more than state it in a single word of utter possession. "Mine."

"Always."

It was enough. For now it would do. His hands swept over her, a burning desire to explore every part of her, to know it quickly and thoroughly. But he couldn't. It wasn't possible. He couldn't hold back long enough and even as he took her, satisfied his initial hunger, he knew it would return. That it couldn't be sated, not tonight. Not anytime soon. One helping would never satisfy him…or her. She called to him, her voice an irresistible siren's song that made him deaf to any and all women—those who came before and those shadows of tomorrow who would never be. On some level he sensed himself incapable of hearing them the way he heard her. Could never respond to them the way he responded to her.

And with that knowledge, he let go. Let go of a lifetime of restraints and caution. Sliced through the Gordian knot of his control. For the first time, he gave himself fully to a woman, holding nothing back. Gave himself up to the fury and passion. He could tell the instant she let go, as well. Heard her cry of surrender, felt the shift as they climbed. Felt that breathless moment of ecstasy as they hovered at the peak. Felt the explosive climax. And then they tumbled into the wild and uncharted.

But he wasn't alone there. He had Angie.

Six

"I gather we're now committed to this course of insanity?" Angie asked, her voice satisfyingly breathless.

Lucius rolled onto his side, facing her. "So it would seem."

Unable to help himself, he traced the length of her neck. Unbelievable how much her skin felt like silk. He glided his fingertips across the hollow at the joining of neck and throat and farther, to the gentle curve of her breast. She shivered at the touch, and with their bodies still intimately linked he could feel the abrupt kick to her heart rate. Instead of being amused by her reaction, it humbled him. His touch alone could do that. And he had a sneaking suspicion her touch alone affected him the exact same way.

Aw, hell. It wasn't supposed to be this way. Sure, he'd hoped for a mutually satisfying sexual relationship. But this felt like more than that. This felt dangerous. Serious. It was time to adjust course, because going down this road led straight to disaster, particularly when Angie had been crystal clear about her disinterest—hell, her distaste—for anything too personal. And after Lisa… Well, he knew better than to look for something that didn't exist.

And yet, still he wanted Angie. Still, he touched. And touching, possessed. She didn't hesitate when he turned to her, gathered her in. Her initial acquiescence became demand, her demand an intriguing combination of uncertainty and aggression. And something else. Something he couldn't quite put his finger on. Then it hit him. Infuriated, challenged, defied him. *Reticence.* She was holding back, refusing to give herself fully to him, and the knowledge drove him wild.

"Look at me," he demanded. He speared his fingers into the thick tumble of her hair, anchoring her so she had no choice but to meet his gaze. "I want you to see who you're in bed with."

A laugh broke from her, a heartbreaking sound. "I see you. I've always seen you."

"You're holding back and I won't have it. I'm not Moretti. I'm not a one-night stand. I'm not some convenient body in the dark you can use for a night's worth of temporary pleasure and then toss aside come morning."

"I know you're not. I've never—" She shook her head, fighting him. "I don't *do* one-night stands."

He throttled back, allowed his voice to go low and soothing. "Then trust me. Let go. I won't hurt you. I swear I won't."

Her eyes sheened with tears and one escaped, sliding down her temple to lose its way in her hair. "You don't understand. I don't think I can. I don't know how."

"Don't think. Just feel."

He slowed the pace, drew out each caress, each kiss. Lingered and wallowed until he felt the slow give of her body. He explored her, the uncharted territory as well as the familiar, delighting in the sleek and toned, tracing from subtle curve to quiet valley. He still sensed a certain resistance, but inch by inch he soothed and encroached his way through her barriers, not giving her time for defense or withdrawal. And all the while he talked to her, a gentle, soothing whisper of words that eased him closer and closer to the true heart of the woman he held.

The instant the last bastion fell, he joined their bodies, one to the other, taking her in every sense of the word, penetrating with one devastating stroke. Her cry of surrender shattered the air and the moment she let go was also the moment she fully awoke. He didn't understand how or why. He didn't understand what past issues had caused such caution, although he swore to himself that he would. He simply matched her. If he'd thought what had come before had been life altering, it bore no comparison to what they now shared. He could only ride the wave with her, fighting to stay ahead of the tumble, to draw out the experience to its ultimate degree. To show her the possible. The impossible. The transcendent.

He had no idea whether they slept afterward. More likely, passed out. When consciousness returned, he found them so tangled together he suspected it would take a herculean effort to separate male from female. She stirred, though she made no attempt to shift away from him or begin the untangling process. He hoped she'd lost the ability to raise any further barricades against him.

"Why?" she asked simply.

"I wanted all of you," he replied just as simply. "I wanted more than you would have given Moretti or any other man."

She shifted, just enough to put a whisper of cool air

between them. "And did you give me more than you gave Lisa or any other woman?"

He didn't even attempt to lie. "Yes." He cupped her cheek—heaven help him, but she had skin like velvet—and leaned in for a slow, thorough kiss. "I didn't plan to. But it only seemed fair, all things considered."

He caught it then, that flash of vulnerability, secrets dimming her eyes to a sunset aquamarine. "I've never found sex fair or safe. I'm not sure it can be."

Ah, finally. He'd gotten to the root of the matter. "I don't disagree, though I'd love to be proved wrong." He paused a beat. "Who was he, Angie?"

Her eyes swept closed in momentary resistance before she looked at him again. One more small surrender. "His name was…is…Ryan. We lived together for a while. We planned to marry."

"And who was she?" Because he didn't doubt for one tiny minute that another woman came between them.

"My best friend, Britt," she confessed. He could hear the effort it took to keep her voice level and dispassionate. "I found them in bed together."

Ah. Which must have struck at the very core of her womanhood. Made her question everything about herself, particularly her own sexuality. Not that she should have any concerns on that front. He released his breath in a long sigh, the similarities between her situation and his resonating more keenly than he'd have liked. "We are a pair, aren't we? Both betrayed. Neither willing to trust. Maybe we can work together to get past all that, assuming we can continue to trust each other."

For some reason his comment caused her to stiffen, a hint of alarm to flicker across her expression. "Lucius—"

"Don't take it personally, Angie. In fact, you're one of the few people I do trust. At least, as much as I trust anyone. You. Geoff. My dad." His mouth twisted when he realized she was the only one left of those he'd named. "Did you ever meet Geoff?"

"Yes," she whispered.

"He was a lot like my dad. Just..." He moved his shoulders in a shrug. "Decent, you know? Down to his bones decent, like Dad. I guess that quality allowed people to take advantage of them both. Unlike me, they weren't suspicious enough. They regarded everyone as a potential friend instead of trying to figure out the angles, figure out what the other person wanted."

"But you always try and figure out the angles. You look for the underlying motivation."

"Every damn time," he confirmed. "My father lost his business because he trusted his business partner. Was blind to Lynley's agenda."

Her gaze traced his face, no doubt looking for a soft place to land. She wouldn't find it. "I heard Lynley took the company from your father."

"The betrayal gutted my father. He wasn't the same man afterward." Lucius swallowed past the acid eroding his throat. "He wasn't bitter like me, nor vengeful. He was...confused and bewildered. And later, hurt beyond measure. After that, he just gave up, let the betrayal kill him."

"They say..." She pulled away from him another inch or two, more than just a whisper this time. "They say you went after Lynley. Took him and his company down. That's how you acquired the nickname Devil Devlin."

He didn't pull his punches. "Guilty as charged. And I'd do it again without hesitation."

"And Lisa?" She withdrew a little farther, widening the breach between them until he could see the beginnings of a chasm. "Did she betray you?"

Had she? He considered, surprised to discover that she hadn't. He'd always known what she wanted. Hell, it hadn't been a secret. "Lisa wanted marriage," he replied slowly. "She didn't particularly care who she married, so long as he possessed a healthy bank account. I was her first choice, but only because I had more money than Geoff. Once she realized I wouldn't marry her, she moved on."

"To Geoff." A frown darkened Angie's expression. "I imagine you felt quite protective toward him. After all, he was your best friend and a lot like your father. Do you think on some level you were determined to save him, especially since you couldn't save your father?"

Lucius had considered the possibility when Lisa first went after Geoff. He suspected it also played a big part in that final night he'd spent with her, and his willingness to bed her one last time. Even though he knew it risked his friendship with Geoff, he'd taken that risk in order to reveal her true nature once and for all. "I tried to get Geoff to see Lisa for what she was. Not that it did any good. In the end it was his choice, his life, and I had to respect that."

"At some point would you have taken her down, too?"

And there it was, the true motivation behind Angie's questions. She feared his ruthlessness, and not without good cause. "No, sweetheart. I never would have touched Lisa, not once she married Geoff." He could tell his blunt, starkly honest response eased her concerns.

"Because you still loved her?"

Unable to help himself, he escaped the bed and put some distance between them. For some reason the question disturbed him, ripped a scab off a wound only half-healed. And then it hit him and he closed his eyes.

"Lucius?" His name contained a hint of uncertainty. "What is it?"

He turned around. Faced her. Found it the height of irony that he stood before her, stripped naked in every sense of the word. "I didn't love Lisa. I loved Geoff. He was my brother in all but blood. He's the reason I'd never have taken her down. Out of respect for him, for what he hoped to build with her." He shook his head, gutted. "It doesn't make any difference, anyway. They're all gone now. My dad. Geoff. Lisa."

"Everyone you loved." He closed his eyes to hold at bay the compassion he read in her voice and expression, rejecting it. "There's still one more person, Lucius. There's Mikey." Urgency raced through her words, hammered at him. "He needs you. He needs your love."

And perhaps that bothered him most of all. "I'm not sure I'm capable of love anymore." He didn't give her time to debate the issue. He checked the clock by his bedside table. "It's getting late. I don't know about you, but I'm starved. I'm going to call for a meal to be brought up. Your choice whether they serve it while you're still naked."

The comment accomplished just what he hoped. It served to catapult Angie out of bed. She hastened around the room, gathering up her clothing. Watching, he had the almost-overpowering urge to snatch all that gorgeous nudity back into his arms and return her to his bed. To make love to her all over again, long into the night, until he'd found a way to sate the desire that continued to infect him, that simmered through his veins and pooled in his loins and demanded he take. Possess. Stamp repeatedly with his possession.

"Do you mind if I grab a quick shower?" she asked, clutching her bundle of clothing to her chest.

He fought to make sense of her words. But all he could

see were those legs. That pearly skin. The tumble of soft curls that haloed her lovely face. Those huge, haunting aquamarine eyes. Silently swearing, Lucius forced his brain into gear, dissected her words one by one and shoved out a response.

"Go ahead."

She turned, presenting him with that perfect, round backside. If she hadn't been moving at such a swift clip, he would have lunged for her. Yanked her back into his arms and his bed and taken her in a helpless frenzy of need.

Mikey. Remember Mikey. The boy had to come first and foremost. He was the only reason Lucius had taken Angie to his bed. Was considering marrying her and making her an intimate part of his life. He must never forget that. Geoff's son came first. The side benefits of marrying Angie were just that. Side benefits. A tasty appetizer to enjoy, but not the main meal. He couldn't allow himself to become distracted by a pert bottom, stunning legs, an elegant face or wary, vulnerable eyes. Eyes that made him want to wrap her up in an endless embrace and protect her against…

Against what?

Himself, he realized. Against using her. Hurting her. Causing her the sort of pain Britt and Ryan had. The sort of pain Lynley had caused his father. The sort of pain, ultimately, Lisa would have caused Geoff simply because it wasn't in her nature to remain faithful to any one person. He needed to remain dispassionate and focused on Mikey, to the exclusion of everything—and everyone—else.

And yet, still he wanted. Yearned. Fought to control what shouldn't matter…but did.

Blistering the air with his frustration, Lucius swiftly dressed, then placed their dinner order. He made a beeline for the living room, aware if he didn't get the hell out of the bedroom—and now—neither of them would leave anytime soon. How was it possible that something so simple had taken such an unfortunate turn?

When he'd first considered using the Pretorius Program to help him find a wife, he'd been determined that his marriage would be one of pure convenience for both parties. That any sexual involvement would remain physical, uncomplicated by any sort of emotional connection—exactly what Angie wanted, which should have made it perfect for them both. In fact, that particular requirement had been one of the most difficult to fulfill, according to the program's designer. For some reason, women entering the marital estate wanted love, something he couldn't and wouldn't offer.

Even when Angie's name had been raised, he'd experienced a swift wash of relief. He'd marry someone he respected, with whom he had a comfortable relationship. A woman he trusted. Someone he wanted sexually and who, based on her response to their kiss after the business dinner with Moretti, wanted Lucius, but without the added obstacle of messy emotional demands, a prerequisite that worked well for them both.

But something had happened when he took Angie to bed. Something he didn't want to examine too closely. Something he didn't dare analyze. Ever. All he knew was that he'd never experienced such perfection with any other woman. Lisa, with whom he'd enjoyed a very passionate, energetic sex life, paled in comparison. And he knew why.

Once he broke through her restraint and Angie gave herself to him, she gave everything, unstintingly, just as he'd demanded. She held nothing back. Every part of her was open to him, gifted to him with a generosity that unmanned him.

Damn it! Hadn't he just promised himself he wouldn't

analyze what made Angie different from the other women he'd known?

She appeared in the doorway between his bedroom and the living room just then and he fought not to laugh at the irony. Angelique, the tempting sex goddess he'd been so busily fantasizing about had been replaced by Ms. Angie Colter, PA Extraordinaire, fully zipped, buttoned and uncreased, from the painfully tight knot of hair at her nape to the sensible heels concealing her pretty painted toes. Despite that, he caught the merest hint of nervousness eroding the edges of her composure.

"Dinner's not here yet?" she asked.

"Not yet." He lifted an eyebrow. "You okay?"

"Fine."

But she wasn't. Not totally. "Except for…?"

Before she could respond, a panel by the elevator buzzed. "I assume that's our dinner," she prompted, her relief almost palpable.

Lucius nodded in confirmation. Fine. He'd save the postcoital interrogation until after dinner. He crossed to the panel in the foyer and punched in a code. A few minutes later the doors opened and a young man in his late teens stepped from the car bearing a cardboard box, a cocky grin and a long golden braid that flowed all the way to his waist. It twitched rhythmically to the music pouring from the earbuds dangling from his ears.

"Thanks for being so prompt, Tuck," Lucius said.

"Anything for you, Mr. D. You want it in the dining room, as usual?"

"If you wouldn't mind."

He started in that direction, his stride catching in a brief hitch when he caught sight of Angie. To Lucius's amusement, he gave her a quick, flirtatious wink before continuing on his way. He made short work of setting up their meal, then returned with the empty box. "Nice one, Mr. D.," he murmured under his breath. "I live to be you."

He handed the kid a generous tip and jerked his head in the direction of the elevator. "Just live to be yourself, Tucker," he advised.

"That was my second choice," the teen replied. Hopping onto the elevator he punched the button for the lobby. Just as the doors slid shut he waggled his brows in Angie's direction and gave her a low wolf whistle.

"Interesting character," she said with a laugh.

"He takes a little getting used to, but he's harmless." Lucius led the way into the dining room and held the chair for Angie. "Smart, too. He received a full scholarship to U-Dub. Wants to be an engineer."

"Did you attend the University of Washington?"

"Yes. Or I did until my father died," he qualified. He selected a bottle of chilled white wine that would mate well with their meal, made short work of opening it. "I dropped out at that point to salvage what I could of his business. Not that there was anything left to salvage. Lynley had gotten it all by then."

"And then you started Diablo, Inc.," she prompted.

"That took a few years to get off the ground." He transferred some chicken stir-fry to her plate. "I think you'll like this. They use an excellent blend of spices."

She took a bite, her startled gaze flashing to his. "Oh, wow."

He smiled. "Told you."

They ate in silence for a few minutes. Drank wine. He watched while she pushed a bite of dinner around her plate, working up the nerve to speak. Finally, she glanced at him and caught him looking. She released a low laugh. "Aren't you going to say, 'Out with it, Colter'? You don't normally show such patience."

He shrugged. "I knew you'd work up to it in a bit. It gave me a chance to eat before you grilled me again."

"I'm not going to grill you. To be honest, I just wondered… Where do we go from here?"

Back to bed, he almost replied, but refrained. She must have guessed the direction of his thoughts, though, because warm color swept across her cheekbones.

"Other than there," she added drily.

He sipped his wine. "Tomorrow's Saturday. We'll spend the day picking out an engagement ring. Make it official. We'll break it to the Ridgeways when we pick up Mikey on Sunday."

"We?" A part of her loved the way he connected them with such ease. Another part struggled to deal with the speed with which they were moving forward. "You want me to come with you?"

"From this point forward, we're joined at the hip," he confirmed. "We present a unified front in every regard. Got it?"

It made perfect sense. The Ridgeways needed time to assimilate the changes. Even more important, they needed time to buy into those changes. To believe without question that she and Lucius were a couple, and would make excellent parents for Mikey. Although, no question, that would take quite a bit of convincing. She nodded in agreement. "Got it."

"Excellent." His cell phone rang just then. He checked the number and frowned. "I better take this. It's the Ridgeways." He connected the call. "Benjamin? Oh, Tabby. Is there a problem? Mikey?"

To Angie's concern, his expression closed over and she stood, crossed to where he sat. Unable to help herself she slid a supportive hand onto his shoulder, praying nothing had happened to the baby.

"We'll be right there." He snapped the cell phone closed. "She thinks Benjamin has had a heart attack. They're at the hospital and she's requested that I pick up Mikey."

"Let's go," she said simply.

"One quick adjustment first." He stood, ran his gaze over her in a manner that had her stiffening. "I'd hoped to have this weekend to set the stage a little better."

For some reason she found herself falling back a step. "What does that mean?"

"It means, when we get to the hospital, try gazing at me adoringly rather than like you are now." At her look of utter confusion, he clarified, "As though I'm about to steal your chastity, run off with the family jewels and give a boot to your little pet dog on my way out the door." He approached, looking entirely too dark and dangerous. "From now on you need to look a bit less professional and a hell of a lot more like my future wife."

Her breath quickened. "Perhaps the engagement ring we purchase tomorrow will be sufficient. Besides, Mrs. Ridgeway will be too distracted by concern for her husband to pay attention to me."

"Don't be so sure, not when it comes to Tabby. She might not consciously notice, but in retrospect she'll pick up on the clues. Assuming we give her a few to pick up on." He paused in front of Angie, so close she could feel his warmth and catch a hint of his scent, a scent he'd somehow imprinted on her in those hours they'd shared in his bed. Before she could stop him, he reached for her hair, tumbled it free of the tidy knot she'd settled for after her shower. "Better."

"Lucius—"

"Much better. Keep saying my name like that and there won't be any question about our relationship."

He reached for her, drew her up for a slow kiss, one that had her melting against him. And then another, deeper, more thorough. She didn't have a clue how long the embrace lasted. Minutes. Forever. When he finally released her she discovered he'd somehow freed the first few buttons of her blouse, exposing the lacy edge of her bra. She fell back a pace, fumbling with the buttons, only to have him stop her.

"Leave it," he ordered.

"You can't expect me to go around like this. What will people think?"

"Exactly what we want them to think. That we're a couple who can't keep our hands off each other. A couple who were caught in bed when Tabby called and threw on the first things that came to hand before rushing off to the hospital."

She could feel warmth burning a path across her cheekbones. "I don't think I can do this."

"You don't have a choice. I don't want there to be any question that our marriage is a love match. I don't want the Ridgeways to have any grounds for suggesting otherwise." He tipped her chin upward, his black eyes burning into hers. "When we rush into the hospital together I want on some level for Tabby to believe we just rolled out of bed."

"Not much of a stretch considering we did," Angie muttered.

His mouth twisted to one side. "Unfortunately, my dear Ms. Colter, you have an innate knack for presenting a calm and unruffled front. Excellent when it comes to a work setting, but not at all what I need right now."

She glared at him in exasperation. "And you think undoing a few buttons and wearing my hair down will change that?"

"It'll help. So will a carefully staged embrace."

She stared at him in open dismay. "Oh, Lucius, no. Not tonight."

"Of course not tonight," he retorted impatiently. "But soon."

"Is that really necessary?"

Irritation flashed across his face. "What the hell difference does it make if the Ridgeways catch us kissing? We will be kissing. In case there's the least doubt in your mind, we'll be kissing on a regular basis. We'll also be sharing a bed from this point forward."

"You're moving too fast."

"Then catch up," he snapped. "I don't have time to go slow with you, not considering this latest development. Nor is there time for you to turn coy at this late date. I explained what I needed going in. And you know damn well what's at stake here."

Angie's chin shot up. "Back off, Lucius. You're pushing too fast, too hard. We're not married, yet."

"Another fact that I plan to change at our earliest possible convenience." He checked his watch and swore. "We need to go. We can argue about this later."

He was right. They did need to go. She held her tongue while he whisked her into the elevator. The ride to the garage level took next to no time. He led her to a new BMW sedan that took her by surprise. She wouldn't have associated the car with him, vaguely recalled he drove something far sportier, until she caught sight of the car seat in the back. It hit her then. He'd purchased the car with Mikey in mind. And she'd bet the title on her pretty little house in Ballard that this particular model possessed one of the highest safety ratings around.

They pulled out into the misty Seattle night, the dampness causing the tires to softly hiss against the pavement.

Darkness clamped down on them, intensifying the intimacy within the confines of the car. To Angie's relief, Friday night traffic proved light, perhaps because it was well past rush hour, also well past the time when people would be heading out for dinner dates or theater engagements. The darkness and intimacy also gave her the courage to address an issue she'd neglected to ask Lucius about, an issue that continued to nag at her. She decided to get it out into the open before committing herself to her role as his fiancée.

"Would you mind if I asked you a question about Mikey and your guardianship of him?"

He spared her a swift glance before returning his attention to the road. "Since you'll soon be his mother, I don't mind at all."

"His mother," she repeated faintly. "I…I hadn't thought of it quite that way."

"Start."

She gave a quick nod. "Okay. I can do that. I think."

"What's your question?"

"Why?" she asked simply. "Why did you agree to take Mikey and why are you so determined to keep him—to the extent of marrying a virtual stranger? Why not just let the Ridgeways have him? It would certainly be simpler."

"Excellent question and one I've asked myself countless times over the past three months." His mouth compressed and a frown of concentration etched a path across his brow. "There are several reasons, to be honest. First, I made a promise to Geoff, and I don't ever—*ever*—renege on my promises."

"There's a reason for that, isn't there? Your father?" she hazarded a guess. "And what happened between him and Lynley?"

"I will never be Lynley," he confirmed. "I will never break a promise, once made."

She didn't doubt him for a single moment. Lucius Devlin might be one of the most ruthless men she'd ever met, but he had a code of honor as inherent and unalterable as the color of his eyes or the hard, uncompromising angles of his face. Even with Lisa, if she and Geoff had still been a couple when she'd come crying on his shoulder, he'd never have laid a finger on her. Angie knew that with utter certainty.

"And your other reasons?" she prompted.

"The Ridgeways aren't fit guardians." He made the statement in a flat, absolute voice. "They despised Lisa, and there's not a question in my mind that Mikey will ultimately pay the price for their attitude toward his mother."

"I agree," Angie murmured unhappily. "Mrs. Ridgeway, in particular, seems almost zealous in her determination to make sure Mikey doesn't take after Lisa in any fashion."

"Lisa had her flaws, but one thing I know for certain. She adored Mikey. She was like a lioness with her cub when it came to her son."

Angie regarded him with grave eyes. "But there's another reason you've decided on this course of action. I can tell."

"That's none of your business," he stated gently.

"I disagree. If I'm to be your wife, if I'm to be Mikey's mother, I think it is my business."

He had zero intention of answering her, she could tell. But then to her utter astonishment, the words escaped in a whispered confession, full of pain and regret, spilling into the heavy darkness of the car.

"Mikey could have been mine."

Seven

Angie stared at Lucius in disbelief. *"What?"*

He flicked her with a brief glance with pit-black eyes, enfolding himself in remoteness.

"Lucius… The timing was that close?" she pressed.

"Yes."

"Did you… Has it occurred to you—"

"That Mikey might be mine? Of course. After Lisa announced her pregnancy I approached her privately and asked. She promised to have a DNA test done after Mikey was born."

"Talk about awkward." Angie caught her lip between her teeth. "I assume Geoff knew about—"

"Our encounter, for lack of a better word? Yes. Our friendship survived it. Barely. After Mikey was born, Lisa was quite up-front about the test. She arranged for it to be conducted, all very discreet and private, all of us very polite and sophisticated about the situation. Geoff was certain Mikey was his. As it turned out, he was right. But that doesn't change anything. I could have been the father just as easily as Geoff. And if our situation were reversed, I would have wanted him to stand for me if I'd orphaned my son. And Geoff would have done it, too. He was that sort of man."

Angie caught the black pain underscoring his words and her heart went out to him. More than anything she wished she could take him in her arms and soothe the hurt. But she couldn't. Not only were they in a moving car, but they didn't have that sort of relationship. She fought back a pained laugh, one she didn't doubt would be edged with hysteria. They'd made love. They planned to marry. But she didn't dare comfort her future husband. Could it get any more bizarre?

They arrived at the hospital just then, putting an end to the conversation. Parking proved more problematic since visiting hours hadn't yet ended. Lucius finally slipped into a space a good hike from the emergency room entrance. Right before they walked through the sliding doors, he annoyed her by giving her hair a quick ruffle, tumbling the curls into just-out-of-bed disorder.

They found Tabby Ridgeway in a jam-packed waiting area. Somehow she held herself aloof from the noise and bustle and misery. She cradled a sleeping Mikey in her arms and sat with her eyes closed, the deep lines carved into her face revealing age and exhaustion and fear in equal measure.

Sensing their presence, she glanced in their direction and drew herself up as though steeling herself, a regal hauteur snapping into place along with her spine. Her gaze shifted from one to the other of them and in that instant Angie realized Lucius had been right. As usual. A woman's awareness filtered through Tabby's obvious distress, one that took in Angie's hair, the not fully fastened buttons of her blouse, the lack of makeup. A hint of outrage flashed through her cold eyes, then was gone.

"How's Benjamin?" Lucius asked. He gently unburdened Tabby, ignoring her instinctive flinch to prevent him from taking the baby. Mikey stretched and opened his eyes, grinning and babbling excitedly when he saw who held him. "Is there anything we can do to help other than take Mikey?"

She registered the word *we* by switching her attention to Angie and narrowing her eyes. "I shouldn't have called. Clearly, I've interrupted something."

"You did. Angie and I were celebrating our engagement," Lucius replied easily. "But don't worry about it. All that can wait. It's not like it's come as any surprise to either of us. We'll celebrate tomorrow when we pick out the ring." He switched his attention to the baby. "You can come along and help us decide which one is best, can't you, little guy?"

"Engaged?" Angie caught the confusion, followed by a reassessment. "You two are engaged to be married?"

Lucius nodded. "It's been in the works for a while." Angie couldn't get over the gentleness of his tone or the effortless way he held the baby, bouncing him in a light, rhythmic motion that spoke of experience in quieting a fussy infant, or entertaining a happy one. "Since she works for me—for the moment—we haven't wanted to say anything. It didn't seem…appropriate."

Angie deliberately changed the subject. "Is there any news about Mr. Ridgeway's condition?"

Fear invaded Tabby's features once again. "Not yet. They're taking so long. Too long."

"Let me see what I can find out." Lucius transferred the baby to Angie. "I'll be right back."

Angie cradled Mikey against her shoulder and took the seat next to Tabby. "If you want to get yourself a drink or some food, I can wait here and watch your things."

"No. No, I don't want anything." She twisted her hands together, waves of disapproval emanating from her. "How long have you and Lucius…?"

Oh, dear. They hadn't discussed the details of their cover story, yet. "About nine months," she improvised, deciding Lucius would want the relationship to predate his guardianship. "We were going to announce our engagement sooner, but…" She trailed off in the hopes that Tabby would assume the announcement had been postponed after Geoff's and Lisa's deaths.

She nodded. "Very considerate of you," she said in a stiff voice. "I'm surprised you'd be willing to take on a man like Lucius, especially now that he has the responsibility of my grandson."

"I adore Mikey. I have from the moment I first saw him."

"We—Benjamin and I—don't feel Lucius is a fit parent."

Angie tiptoed through the minefield which had opened up so unexpectedly in front of her. "Perhaps with time, you'll discover otherwise. I know he has a reputation, but I've found that reputation to be a bit of an exaggeration." She offered a conspiratorial smile. "You know how businessmen are. If people think you're ruthless, they're more respectful and cautious in their dealings with you. I'm sure Geoff would never have appointed Lucius his son's guardian if he didn't have complete faith in his best friend's character."

"Geoff was under the influence of *that woman,*" Tabby retorted. "I'm not sure he was in an adequate frame of mind to judge."

Okay, Angie decided. Clearly, she wasn't going to win this particular argument, not that she'd expected to. Heavy silence settled between them, as chilly and bitter as the breeze that gusted through the sliding doors whenever they parted to cough out a new arrival. She glanced in the direction Lucius had disappeared, relieved to see him striding in their direction, a doctor at his side.

"This is Dr. Sanji," he explained, making the introductions. "He's the cardiologist who's been taking care of Benjamin."

The doctor sat beside Tabby and gathered her hand in his. Brave man, was all Angie could think. "All is well, Mrs. Ridgeway. Your husband did not suffer a heart attack, but a panic attack."

Tabby's chin trembled. "Not his heart? You're certain?"

"Quite certain." His light brown eyes stayed fixed on her, their expression calm and reassuring. "I understand you are both under considerable emotional distress. This weekend would have been your late son's birthday, is that correct?"

Tabby nodded, pressing her lips tightly together. "He would have been thirty-two."

"No doubt this is the root cause of your husband's problem. Panic attacks often mimic the symptoms of a heart attack. The nausea, dizziness, shortness of breath."

"I didn't know what to do," she confessed, "so I called 9-1-1."

"As you should have. We have put him on a mild antianxiety medication, which will ease his distress. You should be able to take him home in a few hours. Until then, why don't you come sit with him?" He offered a charming smile. "I'm sure having you at his side will do far more for him than any medication."

Tabby spared Mikey a worried glance. "My grandson?"

"Don't worry about that." Angie leaped into the breach. "Lucius and I will take good care of him."

Tabby retreated behind her wall of reserve. "See that you do." Sweeping to her feet, she collected her handbag. "Please return the diaper bag the next time we have visitation." She didn't bother waiting for an answer, but stalked away without a backward glance.

"Let's get out of here," Lucius said. "Are you okay with Mikey?"

"If you'll grab the diaper bag, I'm fine." She traced her hand across the baby's soft dark curls. "It's so noisy here, I can't believe he's fallen asleep again."

"He's a good kid, just like his dad." After making sure Mikey was protected against the elements, they exited the emergency room and headed for the car. Lucius hit the remote to disengage the locks. "Did she buy the engagement?" he asked, shooting Angie a searching glance.

"Seemed to."

"Let's see if we can't find a way to shift that to 'completely sold' on the concept." He took Mikey and slipped him into the car seat with the ease of three months' worth of practice. Angie watched carefully while he took care of the various buckles, committing the process to memory in case she was called on to do it in the future. "Let's get home. I don't know about you, but I'm exhausted."

The return trip didn't take long. Mikey woke up just as they were parking the car, his whimpers increasing to wails with each passing minute. The instant they reached the foyer, Lucius inclined his head in the direction of the kitchen. "He sounds hungry. I'll warm up a bottle."

"I'll check his diaper and get him ready for bed."

"His bedroom is opposite mine. Ours," he corrected himself. "You'll find everything you need in there."

She located the room without any trouble. Before

Mikey's advent it had been used as an office. A crib occupied one corner of the room, while a huge mahogany desk had been transformed into a changing table, the surface boxed in with a wooden topper to prevent the baby from rolling off. His pitiful wails eased off the instant she stripped him of his sopping disposable diaper. She'd have been a bit more uncertain about the process if she hadn't had the opportunity to help out with Mikey's care over the past dozen weeks. She hadn't been called on to assist often, just enough to refresh her memory from her babysitting days. With luck, Lucius wouldn't pick up on the fact that she wasn't quite as experienced as her résumé claimed.

To her amusement, she found sleepwear in a gorgeous mahogany file cabinet that matched the desk, clearly repurposed to serve as Mikey's dresser. Fighting flailing limbs, she managed to get him snapped together. Then she scooped him up and carried him into the living room.

A couple minutes later, Lucius entered with a baby bottle. "Want me to take him?"

"I don't mind feeding him." She took a seat on the couch and smiled down at Mikey. "I don't often get the chance."

"That's about to change." He tested the temperature of the milk a final time and handed her the bottle. "A lot of things are about to change."

Mikey latched onto the nipple and she chuckled at his greedy enthusiasm. "At least we got the hard part over with. Now that the Ridgeways know about our engagement, maybe they'll hold off suing for custody."

He turned off the overhead lights, allowing the illumination from the city to bathe the room in a soft glow. "They might hold off. Especially if we follow it with a wedding as soon as possible."

It took a moment for his words to penetrate. The instant they did, her head jerked up and she looked across the room at him. He stood in front of the bank of windows that marched along one full wall of the room, his forearm braced against the glass. He kept his back to her while he stared out at the city. Even though his stance gave the impression of casual indifference, she caught a line of tension sweeping across his shoulders and a dangerous stillness that usually came before the predatory pounce.

"As soon as possible?" she repeated uneasily. "What sort of time frame are we looking at?"

He shrugged, a swift, restless movement. "Days. No more than a week or so."

Angie lifted the baby to her shoulder and rubbed his back, struggling to pinpoint the quality in his voice that sounded off. "Why the rush?" she asked.

He turned to face her. Even then she couldn't read him, his expression buried within the thick shadows consuming the room. "I want this tied up. A done deal."

This time she didn't need to read his expression. She could hear the fierce determination in his voice, the intent lurking beneath the words. "You mean, you want *me* tied up."

"If that's how you prefer we do it next time." A blatantly sexual undertone rippled through his dark voice. "I'm sure I can accommodate you."

"Cut it out, Lucius."

"I don't think I can." He approached, his movements as sleek and graceful as a lion on the prowl. "I want you tied up, tied down, tied to me. I don't want to give you room to escape."

She stared at him in bewilderment. "Who said I planned to escape?"

"I'm committed, Angie. *We're* committed. We just

made the big announcement to the Ridgeways. There's no going back now and I can't take the risk that you might change your mind."

What in the world was going on? "I understand that, and I have no intention of going back or changing my mind."

"I intend to make certain of it. Tomorrow the ring. Monday, we'll apply for a marriage license. I have no idea if there's a waiting period. If so, we wait. If not..." He shrugged. "No point in wasting the opportunity. We can have it over and done with right then and there."

"Over and done with?" She felt her temper slip and slowly stood. Mikey had fallen asleep once again, and without a word, she set the bottle aside and carried him to his crib. She sensed Lucius following, and turning, found him leaning against the doorjamb. "Lights on or off?" she asked crisply.

"Off. There's a night-light that comes on automatically when the sensor registers the darkness."

Sure enough, it flickered to life, a cute little teddy bear, holding its paw to its muzzle in a *shh* gesture. Without a word Angie brushed past Lucius and returned to the living room. There, she spun around to face him.

"I realize I entered this devil's bargain with my eyes wide open when I agreed to take on this new job." She used the final word deliberately, because despite everything he'd said, that's really how he saw it. "And that our marriage isn't what anyone would remotely consider normal. But it isn't something I plan to get over and done with. I won't be rushed. Nor will I be treated with such casual indifference."

"So you do want a few ribbons and bows, despite what you claimed."

It hurt. His callous disregard hurt more than she could

possibly express. And it was her own fault. He'd been totally up-front about what he wanted from their marriage. He hadn't pretended to love her or have any feelings for her other than pure sexual desire.

Anger warred with hurt. "I need you to back off and stop rushing me. I need time to get used to this crazy idea I've agreed to. It hasn't even been twenty-four hours since you asked me to marry you. I'm not sure it's even been six! It's all happening too quickly. I need you to slow down, give me time to adjust."

Frustration flashed across his expression and he paced the length of the room. "Benjamin isn't well. Fortunately, it's not his heart, but it's clear the stress of losing Geoff is affecting him. Affecting them both. If we marry—soon—they may realize they can't argue I'm unfit or that Mikey won't have a stable home life. In addition, they like you. They may conclude that, although it's not what they originally wanted, they can live with our retaining custody if I grant them liberal visitation rights. Maybe they'll finally realize trying to take on a baby at this stage in their life would be too much for them, particularly after Benjamin's anxiety attack."

"All excellent points. That doesn't mean we need to marry first thing Monday. We have time."

"No." He cut her off with a slashing jerk of his arm. "I don't want to give them that time. I want to push forward while—"

"While what, Lucius? While they're weak? Hurting?"

He swore. "Damn it, Angie. I have my reasons for moving up the timeline and they're sound. I expect you to respect my decision without arguing." He thrust a hand through his hair, regarding her with open frustration. "You never gave me this much trouble when you were my PA. Stop fighting me on this."

"Stop pushing." She planted her hands on her hips. "I'm warning you, Lucius Devlin. If you don't want your apprentice/wife to become your ex-fiancée before you even have a chance to buy an engagement ring, I suggest you give me a little breathing room."

For some reason his eyes narrowed and it took a moment for her to realize what had caused his reaction. The instant she did, the breath stuttered in her lungs. Oh, no. No, no, *no.* She'd said *apprentice/wife.* There was only one way she could have known that term. From Jett or Pretorius. How could she have been so stupid? He continued to stare at her and she couldn't look away, trapped within the ice and fire.

"How long have you known?" Soft. Deadly. The slicing flick of a lash.

She didn't prevaricate, didn't dare. "Since last Monday."

"Who told you? How did you find out?" he demanded. The questions came fast and furious, his expression as hard and relentless as his voice. "Why didn't you tell me you knew?"

She eyed him warily. "Jett let it slip. She assumed I knew and I didn't correct her assumption."

"Son of a bitch."

Maybe a bit of damage control was in order. "I didn't mention it to you because I assumed it was personal and therefore none of my business. When you called me into your office today and said you had a business proposition to discuss with me, I began to suspect it had something to do with the Pretorius Program." She wrapped her arms around her waist. "I understand you used a similar program when you hired me."

It was his turn to hesitate and he made a concerted effort to curb his temper. "Yes. It's how you ended up on the short list for a potential wife. Apparently there was a computer glitch and the two programs were linked. It would seem you were the perfect candidate for both positions."

She couldn't help herself. The lies she'd set up with Jett's help caused her to flinch.

He instantly apologized, mistaking the reason for her reaction. "I shouldn't keep referring to our marriage as though it were a job. I'm hoping it'll become far more than that for both of us."

"But not real," she couldn't prevent herself from saying.

"I promised you I wouldn't make any emotional demands on you and I won't." His words took on a tight, impatient edge. "Does that reassure you?"

No, the comment made her want to cry. She was a fool. A total idiot. She'd locked herself into this travesty of a job—because despite what he said, it *was* a job—in the hopes that he would fall in love with her the way she'd fallen in love with him. Not that he ever would. Lucius Devlin possessed far too much self-control to ever allow such a thing.

"So, where do we go from here?" Angie asked.

He didn't hesitate. "Forward."

She nodded. "Okay." She dared to approach, to run her hand along the impressive ridge of muscles lining his arm. "I promise I'll go through with our marriage, Lucius. I promise I won't back out. All I'm asking is that we take this a little slower. Just a little."

"Tomorrow the ring?"

She nodded. "And Monday we'll take care of the marriage license. That way we're ready should the need arise sooner than anticipated. Fair enough?"

She felt his tension drain away, the muscles beneath her hand gradually relaxing. "I can live with that." He hesitated, then added, "You should have told me you knew about the Pretorius Program."

"You're right. I should have." Time to put a quick end to the conversation before he had time to think of any more questions. She made a point of checking her watch. "It's late. I should head home."

"Excellent idea." Then he surprised her by swinging her into his arms. "Welcome home."

She couldn't help laughing. "Lucius, seriously. I need to go."

He shouldered his way into his bedroom. Depositing her onto the bed, he followed her down. "Trust me, my lovely Angelique, when it comes to having you in my home—and in my bed—I'm dead serious."

And then he consumed her.

"Your assistant has a big mouth, Pretorius."

"She's...young. I'll speak to her."

"Fortunately, the person she slipped up with is Angie, who's discretion personified. If it had been anyone else..."

"Yeah, yeah. Got that." Pretorius hesitated. "The important question is, has the Colter woman agreed to marry you? On paper she's perfect. More than perfect, in fact."

"Amazingly, she has agreed," Lucius confirmed.

"An unusual woman."

No question about that. "One of a kind."

"Sort of surprising she'd go along with the plan this fast. Not something most women would do, as you've discovered for yourself, especially when you're not interested in a..." Pretorius groped for a word both appropriate, as well as tactful. "A traditional marriage. Yeah, that's it. Traditional. You must have offered quite an incentive package."

Lucius hesitated, his eyes narrowing. "Not really."

In fact, now that he thought about it, the terms were heavily weighted in his favor. He attempted to run through their conversation in his office, when he'd first outlined their devil's bargain, as she'd referred to it. Why *had* she agreed? Money? Maybe that played a part in it, though she'd never betrayed any avaricious traits before. And he'd have noticed. A man in his position possessed impeccable radar when it came to greedy women.

Career advancement? Also unlikely. She'd be tied to him for the next five to six years, caring for house and home. Not the smartest way to advance your career, regardless of the payout at the end of their contract. She'd need to retrain. Work her way back up the corporate ladder. Even with his assistance, that would take time. He'd always sensed she took pride in her abilities on the work front. That it was somehow tied to her self-esteem and sense of overall accomplishment. Why give that up to become a wife and mother?

So, why had she agreed to his proposal? He couldn't actually remember her ever saying.

"I've got to go," he informed Pretorius, a trifle abruptly. "Speak to your assistant about her discretion issues. Or should I say, indiscretion?"

"Will do. And congratulations. I hope you and Ms. Colter will be very happy together."

Lucius hung up the phone and glanced toward the elevator. When he'd left his bed, Angie had still been out cold. And with good cause. They'd made love into the deepest, richest part of the night, entwined in passion, then in sleep, lost in an endless embrace as the star-studded inkiness of the dark released its hold to the burning reds and purples of a new dawn. It was as though neither of them could get enough of the other. Even when sleep claimed them they'd remained locked together, craving the intimacy that came through touch and scent.

He crossed to the elevator and returned to his apartment. Angie's voice came from the direction of the kitchen and he found her there with Mikey. The baby sat cushioned in a high chair, and it seemed to Lucius that his balance improved by the day. She offered him a bite of cereal mixed with mashed banana, laughing when he grabbed the spoon and attempted to feed his cheek.

"Close, but no cigar, champ," Angie informed him, gently wiping him clean with a damp washcloth.

She took renewed aim at his gaping mouth, allowing him to assist, and this time the food found its way home and he ate as if they'd been starving him. She must have heard or sensed Lucius's presence because she glanced over her shoulder and smiled. "Morning."

"I'm sorry he woke you," Lucius said. "I planned to feed and change him, but thought I had time to make a quick phone call first."

"No problem. I found the list of safe foods for him on the refrigerator and took it from there."

"It's a system Keesha and I worked out."

"Smart."

Angie wore one of his T-shirts and a pair of sweat shorts he used for workouts. The black cotton tee was too big for her, the neckline slipping off one narrow shoulder. It made her appear even more delicate and feminine. Fine-boned and fragile. Someone to protect the way he needed to protect Mikey. She hadn't taken time to brush her hair and the tousled curls tumbled down her back. She shoved absently at them, hooking the strands behind her ears, not realizing she'd smeared a bit of cereal and banana on her cheek.

Lucius steeled himself against a sight that impacted in

the region of a heart he'd thought long dead. Steeled himself against the craving to take. To hold. To safeguard.

"Why did you agree to marry me?" he asked abruptly.

Eight

For a split second Lucius caught a glimmer of panic in Angie's expressive eyes.

Then she laughed. "Pity."

He struggled to process the word. *"What?"*

"Yup, it's true." She turned back to Mikey. "I was overwhelmed with pity. Poor you. Couldn't even buy yourself a wife. Thank goodness I felt sorry for you or you'd still be trolling for a bride."

"You're marrying me because you *pity* me?"

She released a sigh. Standing, she cleared away Mikey's breakfast. After rinsing the washcloth she'd used to wipe his face, she returned and gave him a gentle scrubbing, one that had him crowing in vehement protest. She released him from his high chair, swept him up and dumped him into Lucius's arms.

"Why don't you get him ready to go outside while I shower? I'd like to swing by my house and change, pick up some clothes to stash over here before we shop for an engagement ring." She waggled her left hand at him. "You do remember you were going to stick a rock on my finger, don't you? And it better be an impressive one. I have a reputation to uphold as Mrs. Lucius Devlin. Because, apparently, not only do I pity you, I'm greedy as hell."

With that, she turned on her heel and presented him with her pert backside showcased by his sagging, oversize sweat shorts. He couldn't help grinning. "She gets high marks for the exit line," he informed Mikey. "Afraid we'll have to deduct points for the shorts, though if she twitched those hips any more she wouldn't have a pair of shorts to worry about."

Then it occurred to him that she hadn't answered his question, which caused him to wonder. Damn it all, why *had* Angie Colter agreed to marry him?

The day sped by. After filling the trunk of his BMW with Angie's possessions, they returned to Seattle's jewelry district to shop for a ring. After the fifth store and an odd reluctance on Angie's part to settle on one, he tugged her into his arms with a growl of exasperation.

"Try showing more greed and less pity," he ordered, drawing her up for a swift, thorough kiss.

She gave herself up to the unexpected embrace without the least hesitation or reticence. He couldn't explain it. How had they gone from a polite working relationship to one so sexually charged that even in the middle of a busy Seattle sidewalk he couldn't keep his hands off her? It didn't make the least sense. He was marrying her for Mikey's sake. Because she was the perfect, most logical choice for a temporary mate. She was intelligent. Gorgeous. Sensible. Sexy as hell. And he wanted her more than he'd ever wanted any other woman.

The intensity of his feelings were dangerous, he acknowledged, and he'd better find a way of throttling back—and fast—or he'd find himself in deep, deep water with no land in sight. He deliberately released her and stepped back. She continued to stand with her eyes closed, swaying for a moment before her lashes fluttered and she looked at him, dazed. It was almost too much to resist. Almost.

"What was that for?" she asked, pressing her fingertips to her swollen mouth.

He had no idea. None. "A reminder," he improvised.

"Okay. Um... What was I supposed to remember again?"

"To pick a damn ring. Make it snappy, Colter. You've always been a reasonable, decisive woman. What is it about an engagement ring that's had you go all...all female on me?"

She lifted an eyebrow, the passion draining from her eyes, replaced with a crisp, cool look of displeasure. "I *am* female, in case you haven't noticed."

"Oh, I noticed," he murmured. That was the problem. He spent entirely too much time noticing.

Her eyes only narrowed, the comment not helping his cause any. "When I see the ring I like, trust me, Lucius Devlin. Your credit card will go from subzero to blazing hot in one fast swipe."

If she hadn't opened the door to the next jewelry store, and stalked inside, he'd probably have kissed her again. He didn't know another human being alive who faced him down with such ease and with such a wicked edge to her tongue. Who would have guessed he'd appreciate that particular quality in a woman? Lisa had always attempted to get her way through wiles. Other women through sex. Still others, with tears. But not Angie. He always knew right where he stood with her. Unfortunately, right now he stood square in the middle of the proverbial doghouse.

He jostled Mikey's stroller through the door and lifted an eyebrow. Did she realize she'd just walked into the Seattle branch of Dantes? He doubted she had any idea what a Dantes original wedding ring cost or she'd have walked by. Hell, she'd have sprinted past. He found her examining a display case, a salesman standing at a discreet distance, ready to assist if needed.

"See anything you like?"

"I'm looking," she said, the words having enough bite that the salesman's eyes widened.

Lucius attempted to look suitably henpecked. "Yes, dear," he murmured. "I'll just take care of the baby while you make up your mind."

Her head jerked up at that and she swiveled, spearing him with a look. Then her anger dissolved and she burst out laughing, utterly confusing the clerk. "See that you do," she ordered with impressive arrogance, falling into the character she'd been assigned. She switched her attention to the display case and pointed. "I'd like to see this one, please."

Lucius came up beside her. "Don't be so polite," he whispered in her ear. "You'll spoil his image of you."

She turned her head, her lips zeroing in on the side of his face in response. Time slowed and he heard the soft give and take of her breath. Inhaled the light fragrance that was so uniquely hers. Felt the faintest brush of her smooth, silken cheek against his more abrasive one. She said something in return. Something that took forever to slip from ear to brain for analysis and interpretation.

"Right back at you, ace. Henpecked husbands-to-be are required to stand a full pace behind their Bridezillas."

She looked at the ring the salesman removed from the

locked display and shook her head. "Close, but not quite what I'm looking for," she confessed. "I don't suppose you have any more by this designer?"

Lucius took a quick look at the ring. Beautiful, of course, considering it was one of Dantes, but definitely not right for Angie. Time to drop the subservient act. He removed a business card and handed it to the salesman. "We'd like to see what you have in the Dantes Exclusive line," Lucius instructed crisply.

The salesman took his card, glanced at the name and stiffened. "Yes, sir, Mr. Devlin. Right away, sir. Mr. Arroya will see to you personally. He's the manager. If you'll just give me a minute to arrange for a showing?"

"We'll wait."

Angie watched the byplay with a small smile of bemusement. "No more role-playing?" she asked.

"No more role-playing," he confirmed. "Tell me what you didn't like about the ring."

"It was elegant, but a little too flowery." She gave an uneasy shrug. "It's probably close, though. Maybe we should go ahead and take this one."

"It's one of the wedding lines created by Francesca Dante, aimed for the average consumer. I think you'll find some of her exclusive collections more to your liking. I should have thought about coming here first."

Angie stirred uneasily. "Exclusive collections?" she repeated. "That sounds pricey. The ring I chose is close enough. I don't mind—"

He cut her off without hesitation. "I do mind." He softened his words by linking their hands. "Your instincts are right on, Angie. You need something elegant, but stunning. Something that makes a statement, and yet suits your personality. People will judge your worth, as well as your value to me, by the ring you choose."

He'd shocked her. "That's horrible."

"I agree, but it's life. Trust me on this."

The salesman returned and escorted them to a sweeping staircase. Lucius removed Mikey from his stroller, while Angie slung the diaper bag over her shoulder with the sort of loving panache that would have befitted a Fendi handbag. Once upstairs, they were shown into a private room with a view of the city.

The room, accented with a wealth of plants and gorgeous fresh flower arrangements, featured a plush, ankle-deep carpet in a pearl gray, giving the impression of luxury combined with warmth. They were shown to a sitting area that consisted of a love seat covered in a discreet pinstripe of gray and white, accented with narrow bands of black, and silk chairs in a rich ruby red. A glass table fronted the love seat and chairs, positioned slightly higher than a conventional coffee table. Overhead spots creating brilliant puddles of light, focused on the table in order to showcase the merchandise.

"I informed Mr. Arroya that the lady finds our Francesca designs most appealing," the salesman explained to Lucius. "He's selecting a few of her pieces with that in mind. In the meantime, may I offer you refreshments? Wine? Champagne?"

"Champagne sounds perfect," Lucius replied, positioning Mikey so he couldn't grab at anything harmful. Not that he need worry. Mikey simply stared at his surroundings, occasionally offering a babbling commentary in a serious tone, one Lucius answered in an equally serious tone.

The salesman returned almost immediately with a silver tray service that included a selection of hard cheeses, a dish of berries and even a small plate of sushi. He opened the champagne, poured. Then indicated the accompanying food. "Shall I serve you or would you prefer some privacy?"

Lucius inclined his head. "We're good, thanks."

The instant he left, Angie turned dazed eyes in Lucius's direction. "Okay, wow."

He handed her a flute. "Get used to it, at least when we're out in public. In private, I prefer leading a far simpler lifestyle."

She helped herself to some cheese, nibbling in what he took to be a nervous manner. "I hadn't thought… Didn't anticipate—"

"You've been part of my life for eighteen months, Angie. You've seen this side of things."

"To a minor extent, yes." She closed her eyes and confessed, "I'm feeling a bit out of my depth."

"You'll get used to it."

She impressed him by nodding, straightening in her seat and taking a deep, calming breath. "Okay, I can handle this." She studied the tray. "Would you like something to eat? The fruit mixture looks incredible."

"Are there currants in there?"

"Yes, and color me impressed that you even know what a currant looks like."

"No choice but to learn. Either that or make sure I carry around a supply of antihistamines."

She regarded him in surprise. "You're allergic to gooseberries? How could I have worked for you for so long and not known that?"

"It's a mystery. I thought you knew everything."

She offered a casual shrug. "I do now. I assume you're not allergic to sushi and cheese?"

He took the plate she offered. "That I can handle."

Tomas Arroya joined them just then, accompanied by an assistant. They exchanged the requisite amount of small talk before getting down to business. He had to give Angie credit. Even though this world was miles out of her realm, she handled it with a quiet poise that impressed the hell out of him.

She took her time examining the rings on display. He was probably the only one to catch the slight hitch in her voice and uncontrollable tremor of her hand when he slipped each ring on her finger. He could also tell that none of the choices was quite right, and sensed she teetered on the verge of choosing one, any one, just to be done with it. Mr. Arroya proved equally astute.

"These all look lovely on you, Ms. Colter," he said gently. "But none suit the way Francesca would insist they must."

"Oh, but—" Angie started to say.

Arroya simply shook his head. "No, no. They won't do. Tonya, bring me Utter Perfection." He patted Angie's hand. "I think this next one may work. It wasn't designed as an engagement ring, but as part of a set. Even so, I suspect it might be right for you."

Tonya returned with a large velvet box. Tomas gestured toward Lucius and the assistant offered him the box. Fire diamonds shimmered beneath the light, exploding in shards of flame in a manner unique to the stones. The pieces were utterly exquisite—a necklace, bracelet, earrings and ring. The sheer simplicity of them would have caused most women to pass over the set in favor of something more ostentatious. But the instant he saw it, he knew it was not only Utter Perfection, but utterly perfect for Angie.

Lucius removed the ring from the case and took Angie's hand in his. Sliding the narrow band of white gold onto her finger, he nodded. "This is the one. We'll take them."

He shot Arroya a look, one that had the manager's eyebrows shooting skyward and had him nodding in instant understanding. Angie remained oblivious to the byplay, one hundred percent of her focus on the ring he'd selected.

"It's...it's the most beautiful ring I've ever seen," she murmured.

And it was. The ring had a curving flow of small, perfect fire diamonds that seemed to float across her finger, like a trail of stars across the night sky. On one side of the pathway of diamonds was a huge, stunning solitaire, set slightly off center. Balancing it on the opposite side was a brilliant sapphire, the two stones like a pair of dancers, twisting around each other across the cosmos, their passage marked by the trail of diamond stars.

It was as unique and individual as the woman on whose finger he'd placed the ring. Even Mikey appeared riveted by the brilliant sparkle, babbling his excited approval. "I couldn't agree more," Lucius said and lifted Angie's hand. He kissed her fingertips, then her mouth. A hint of tears flavored the kiss, revealing one more intriguing facet of her personality. He had a feeling the next few years would prove fascinating as he worked his way through all the interesting layers that comprised the woman soon to become his wife.

"Thank you, Lucius," she said. "It's the most gorgeous ring I've ever seen. Perfect, of course. Utter perfection." She laughed through her tears and held out her hand to admire the flash and burn. Where before there'd been the slightest of tremors, now they visibly trembled.

Lucius's gaze shifted from the ring to the confused delight reflected in Angie's expression. He didn't think he'd ever been with a woman quite so open in her attitude and responses. It pleased him. It more than pleased him. And he was glad they'd taken the time to find the perfect ring.

The perfect ring for the perfect woman, came the wayward thought.

"You're quite welcome, sweetheart. Here..."

He handed Mikey to her while he arranged for payment. She took the baby into her arms and hugged him close while he followed the manager to another room where the business end of the transaction could be completed. The sale was accomplished as discreetly as everything else. Fortunately, the ring didn't require sizing, so Angie could wear it home. He arranged to have the rest of the set messengered to him the next week since he preferred not to walk out the door carrying jewelry that cost the equivalent of a medium-size South Pacific island. Maybe even a small European country.

He rejoined Angie a short time later, and found her leaning against the back of the love seat with her eyes closed. Her left hand cradled Mikey's head, her fingers sinking into the short, dark curls and gently stroking. For some reason, seeing his ring on her finger, the baby he'd taken as his own held tight within the warmth of her embrace, stirred a deep, relentless craving to make the picture she created more than just a business contract.

He felt the image of her and Mikey imprint itself on his mind and on what remained of his heart. And he wanted. Wanted to have the life that image promised. Wanted it to be real. Wanted it to last forever. He backed away, forcing himself to reject a temptation he didn't dare surrender to.

He'd made a promise to her—that he wouldn't force her into an emotional relationship, and he was honor bound to keep that promise. Besides, he wasn't after an emotional involvement any more than she was. Opening himself up, meant trusting. And trusting meant eventual pain and disillusionment. Better to remain above all that, to avoid the bitter fall that would inevitably come if he were foolish enough to succumb to the fantasy.

Deliberately, he turned his back on possibility. "We're done here," he announced.

And that said it all.

He'd been quiet. Far too quiet for Angie's peace of mind.

She glanced up from her book and studied Lucius. He sat on the opposite end of the couch, papers piled around him, Mikey on his lap. It never ceased to amaze her how at ease he was with his parental duties. And yet…

She sensed something, something that worried at the edges of her mind. She'd noticed it on several occasions and tried to call them to mind in the hopes of finding the connecting thread that ran through whatever it was that bothered her. The first time had been before he'd offered her the job of "wife," though not long before, three months after accepting guardianship of Mikey. They'd just finished up work for the day and Keesha had dropped off the baby. As always, the baby greeted Lucius with a huge grin, reaching eagerly for the man he'd someday call "Dad."

And Lucius had grinned back, actually crossing to the sitting area to give Mikey some one-on-one attention. She stood in the doorway to his office, resting her shoulder against the doorjamb while she watched, unnoticed. Since he'd inherited Mikey, she'd discovered that they had a little routine. First, Lucius would tickle Mikey's belly which elicited gales of gurgling laughter. Then he'd play a quick game of peekaboo. And finally, he'd do something that caused an aching tightness to grip her throat. He'd count fingers and toes, as though reassuring himself everything was still safe and sound and accounted for.

This time was no different, except when he started to

pull off Mikey's tiny Seahawk football socks, he stopped and shook his head. And she could see, bit by bit, the way he closed down. Briskly, he checked Mikey's diaper, handed him his favorite rattle and slipped him into his bouncy chair, one guaranteed to keep a baby entertained by playing a dozen different songs and featuring an overhead mobile of various farm animals. It even—heaven help her—vibrated.

The second time had been tonight at dinnertime. He'd taken Mikey into the kitchen to feed him and she'd been highly amused by the noises emanating from that direction. Sounds of planes, trains and cars. Baby giggles. Mealtime was clearly bonding time for the two boys.

And yet, after several moments the tenor had changed and when she entered the kitchen under the pretext of fixing coffee, she discovered it had become all business. Lucius sat with a cool, remote expression on his face, making steady inroads into shoveling food from plate to mouth, while Mikey watched with huge, painfully serious dark eyes.

Angie turned a page in the book she was pretending to read and continued to surreptitiously study the two men her life now revolved around. Where before Lucius had been playing with Mikey, now he studied a contract. She wouldn't have thought anything of it if she hadn't happened to glance up at the exact moment Lucius had transitioned from play to business. And then it hit her.

It was as though he'd caught himself doing something he shouldn't. He'd gone from unselfconscious pleasure to abrupt awareness in the blink of an eye. And in that split second of time he'd barricaded himself off, distancing himself not only from his actions, but from whatever emotions he experienced while interacting with Mikey.

Why? Why would he do that?

He'd also barricaded himself off from her, she suddenly realized. It was after he'd paid for the ring. Up until then, he'd been involved. Engaged. Connected and connecting. She'd assumed the abrupt withdrawal had been the result of the ring costing more than he'd wanted to spend. But now she couldn't help wondering if there weren't another reason altogether.

Maybe he'd allowed himself to become emotionally compromised. Maybe he'd allowed himself, for one short moment, to believe their engagement was real. She couldn't help but wonder if on some level he possessed a sort of internal warning sensor, one that went off whenever he became too personally involved—even if that involvement was with a small, helpless baby.

Even if that involvement was with the woman he intended to marry.

Not that it changed anything. She'd seen the true heart of the man and sensed the depths of emotion he worked so hard to deny. It was because he possessed those depths that he built walls to protect himself, locked himself safely away so he didn't have to feel. Didn't have to suffer the pain of loss or disillusionment.

She had a choice. She could allow him to continue to cement barriers in place until he became so swift and experienced at the process that she'd never find a way to break through. Or she could start undermining those barriers right here and now.

She made her choice even before the options were fully considered. Tossing aside her book, she crossed to where he sat and picked up the sleeping baby. In no time she had Mikey changed and tucked into bed. Then she returned to the living room and turned out the lights, just as Lucius had done the night before. And there, caught within the soft city glow and glitter, she slowly, tantalizingly removed her clothing, piece by piece.

Once again, she couldn't see his expression. But she heard the tenor of his breathing change. Heard it deepen, thicken, grow heavy with desire. And she smiled. When had it happened? When had she lost her nervous dread, her insecurity about satisfying a man? She stood before him wearing only a tiny scrap of silk and lace clinging to her hips and reveled in her femininity, knowing that Lucius wanted her above all women. Not just for her body, though he'd left her in no doubt how he felt about that. But for her intellect, for her personality. And soon, if she had any say in the matter, for her heart.

"Finish it," he practically growled.

She laughed, the sound soft and low. Ripe. Womanly. She skated her hands down her hips and shimmied free of the last of her clothing. And then she stood before him wearing nothing but the ring he'd placed on her finger, the flash a beacon calling him home. She traced her hand across the slight curves of her breasts, allowing the diamond's fire to beckon. Traced her hand downward over her belly to the shadowed valley between her thighs where the fire became a flame.

With a muttered oath, he shot from the couch and caught her in his arms, tumbling her to the thick carpet at their feet. They fought through his clothing, his hands and hers colliding. Tearing. Ripping. Desperate to feel flesh against flesh. And when they were both stripped bare, open and vulnerable, one to the other, they came together.

"No more walls between us," she demanded. "No hiding. No barriers. Just the two of us, allowing the other in."

He shook his head. "It's not what you want." He nuzzled her breast, captured her nipple between his teeth and gently tugged. "Not what either of us wants. We're too damaged to open ourselves like that again."

She shuddered beneath the delicate touch. "How can you say that when this is what happens whenever we make love?" The words hung within the softness of the night, powerful and bright against the darkness. "It *is* what I want. What you want. What we both want from each other. To try again. To feel again. Admit it."

His fingers danced low, sliding into the source of her heat and making her moan in longing. "You're not Lisa…I get that. You're not like any other woman I've known. But I lost the capacity to feel long ago."

How could he say that? He tried to be that dispassionate man, no question. But he was so much more. She'd seen it. Sensed it. "Are we going to live like strangers for the next half-dozen years? Opening ourselves physically, but nothing more? Is that what you want for yourself? For Mikey?" She trailed her hands across the dips and ridges of his abs, following the crisp curls that guided her downward. He was hard and slick, the epitome of masculine strength and virility. She circled his length, guiding him to her heat. "Or do you want everything, everything I have to give?"

Lucius shook his head. "I can't give what I don't have," he claimed.

And yet… And yet she felt the slip. The reluctant easing. The subtle collapse of barriers shifting and trembling. It wasn't a surrender. But it was a start. They had time. Endless time to transition from a place of hurt and suspicion to trust and certainty.

She lifted her hips, took him in, crying out at the sheer perfection of fit and rhythm. "Lucius!" His name became both prayer and demand.

He took her mouth in an endless kiss, then pulled back

ever so slightly. "Look at me. I want you with me on this ride."

Their gazes met, clung. And what she saw there gave her hope. A spark. Just a spark of it, but it was enough. She let go, gave herself up to the heat and fire that burst into life whenever they came together. The flame became an inferno, unstoppable in its power. Branding them. Joining them. Binding them, one to the other—the fit, utter perfection.

Possibilities. He'd stopped believing in possibilities so very long ago.

Lucius gathered Angie up in his arms and carried her to their bedroom. *Theirs.* He shook his head, amused by the speed with which he'd transitioned from "his" to "theirs." And he could pinpoint precisely when it had all changed. It had stopped being his bedroom the first night she'd shared his bed, just as he'd stopped being alone that very same night.

He'd resisted involvement. Would probably continue to resist...for now. But he could see that this time, because of this woman, his life would never be the same again.

She'd shown him a road he'd never noticed before, was utterly surprised to find it beneath his feet and himself some distance along its path. He hadn't anticipated that occurring. Would have vehemently denied the possibility of it ever happening. And yet, here he stood with a woman in his arms and a longing in his heart he hadn't felt in...

Forever.

Possibilities. For some reason his life had become filled with endless possibilities and they were all because of one woman. The woman who wore his ring on her finger. And if he had anything to say about it, it was a ring she'd continue to wear for the rest of her life.

Nine

"I realize this is bad timing, but I have a business trip to New York that I can't postpone," Lucius announced one morning over Sunday breakfast.

To his relief, Angie nodded, not revealing any hint of concern that she'd be left in charge of Mikey and the home front. She poured herself a cup of tea and took a seat beside him. "The Tobias project, I assume?"

"It's reached a crucial point and I need to meet with the investors before moving forward with it."

She took a sip of tea and sighed in unconscious pleasure. He noticed she always did that with her first sip, made that soft, semimoan that caused him to clench his muscles in helpless want. No doubt it had something to do with the ecstatic expression that slid across her face when she drank. He recognized it as a pale reflection of how she looked when he made love to her, the resemblance just close enough to tempt him to sweep her into his arms and closet them in his bedroom for the next several hours. Maybe he'd get used to his reaction to her, to the relentless desire that filled him whenever he looked at her. Maybe he wouldn't respond to that sigh each and every morning for the rest of his life. Maybe. Though somehow he doubted it.

It had been two weeks since they'd become engaged. Two incredible weeks during which, with a fast assist from the Pretorius Program, he'd put a new PA in place, freeing Angie to slip seamlessly into her new responsibilities. Granted, the new PA wasn't Angie, but the motherly woman would do.

When it came to his home life, he couldn't quite get over how well he and Angie fit together, blended, and he'd realized a few days earlier that he no longer thought of their engagement as a position he'd hired her to fill. He couldn't say when the transition had occurred. Like everything else about Angie's advent into his life, it had been equally seamless. He simply recognized that life was different. Better.

He could even fool himself into believing their engagement had come about the way normal engagements did—with two people falling in love and deciding to link their lives through marriage. And though he wouldn't go so far as to claim they'd fallen in love, they'd certainly fallen in lust. Even more important, they enjoyed each other's company. Respected one another. There was such an amazing naturalness to their interactions, a comfortable fit to how their lives had blended. And yet they could exchange a single glance and have passion explode instantaneously between them.

He removed Mikey's breakfast dishes and dumped them in the sink before grabbing one of the neatly folded washcloths on the counter. "I also wanted to warn you that, according to my sources, the Ridgeways still plan to file for custody." He dampened the washcloth and returned to the table to apply it to Mikey's hands and face, ignoring the baby's squirming protests at his mistreatment. "I want our wedding to take place before that happens so no one can accuse us of marrying as a countermeasure."

"You have sources who have inside information regarding the Ridgeways and their lawyer?" At his bland stare, she nodded. "Okay, I guess you do. Why are they delaying?"

"They've arranged for a cardiac specialist to give Benjamin a full workup."

"So you won't have grounds to argue any possible health issues impeding their ability to raise Mikey," she surmised.

"Shrewd as always," he said with an approving nod. "That's precisely their plan."

"Okay." She lifted her shoulder in a casual shrug. "How do you want to handle the wedding?"

The level of relief Lucius experienced at her immediate understanding and willingness to fall in with his plan, caught him off guard. He'd anticipated her arguing the need to marry quite so soon, had his arguments lined up like little ducklings following the mama duck. Or in this case, the papa. He'd been determined to bend her to his will with logic and reason, and if that didn't work, with emotion. He'd even been prepared to commit the ultimate sacrifice and take her to bed and wring an agreement from her once he had her naked and helpless and vulnerable to his influence. Of course, considering those moments of ecstasy left him equally naked and helpless and vulnerable to *her* influence, put him at a small disadvantage. Not that it mattered.

Bottom line, he wanted Angie tied to him in every possible way, wrapped up in inescapable bonds, though he didn't want to look too closely at whether it was strictly for Mikey's sake or if there were another, more personal reason for the sudden rush.

"I'd prefer a small, private ceremony," he said. "Tasteful, with a few close friends and family invited." A sudden thought struck him. "You've never mentioned your parents. Will they attend?"

She shook her head. "My father walked out on my mother when I was Mikey's age. Mom died in a car accident shortly before I started working for you." Her smile held a heartbreaking stoicism. "There's just me."

"I'm so sorry, Angie."

"That's okay."

But it wasn't. He could see it wasn't. One more abandonment. One more relationship that had slipped away, never to be recovered. Could they be any more alike?

"I do have a couple of friends I'd like to include if that's acceptable," she continued. "Trinity, in particular. She's my best friend."

"Of course. Anyone you want. How about a sunset ceremony followed by a small dinner reception? Would that appeal?"

"Very much." Her smile was radiant. "Will you be inviting the Ridgeways?"

"Definitely, though I doubt they'll attend. I'm thinking engraved invitations, the Dorchester Chapel for the service, followed by a private dinner for our guests at Milano's on the Sound. Joe has a room for events like these above the main dining room."

"I'll get on that right away."

She immediately fell into PA mode, opening a kitchen drawer and rummaging around for a pen and notepad.

Lucius took them from her and tossed them aside. Then he drew her into his arms. "You're not my PA anymore."

She settled into the embrace, releasing her breath in a laughing sigh. "That's a good thing since I don't believe our antics last night fall under the heading of proper office decorum."

"Not in any office I've been in charge of." He kissed her, tasting the tea that flavored her lips. "Nor any office I haven't been in charge of."

She settled into his embrace, her trim curves growing more familiar by the day, even as they grew more tempting. "I can't begin to tell you how relieved I am to hear you say that. So, when are you thinking we should marry? I can't send out engraved invitations without a date."

"Good point." He frowned in concentration. "Let me call Joe regarding the dinner and make the arrangements with Dorchester Chapel. I think they'll both be willing to accommodate me."

She stroked her fingers along the jutting curve of his jaw, causing his blood to heat. How did she manage that with just a single touch? "They'll be accommodating because it's you?"

He laughed, the sound ironic. "No, more because of my bank account. It does come in handy at times like this. Once I have that set up, do whatever it takes short of offering sexual favors to get those invitations printed and out as quickly as possible."

She tempted him with a laughing pout. "And here I was looking forward to offering sexual favors."

He chuckled. "You can offer them to me, instead. Or maybe I should offer them to you out of sheer gratitude."

"I have to admit, I like a grateful man," she teased. "Once the venue's set, I'll take care of the rest of the details."

"Thank you, Angie." He couldn't help himself. He took her mouth in a slow, thorough kiss. He vaguely heard Mikey squeal in approval, banging his hands against his high chair tray as though in applause. "I agree, munchkin. That definitely deserved a round of applause."

As always, it took Angie a few seconds to surface and her open passion and lack of artifice never failed to humble him. She moistened her lips as though still tasting him. "You leave tomorrow, right? Monday? How long did you say you were going to be gone?"

"Five days. I'll see if I can't cut it to four. Three. Maybe I can rearrange my schedule and get back here in three."

"I'll see what I can get accomplished in the meantime." She lowered her head to his chest and held on as though it hurt to let go. "Why don't you leave me the key and directions to your Lake Washington house. I'll swing by and start working on some preliminary ideas on that front."

"Do you think you'll have enough time?"

Angie looked up at him and what he read in those soft, aquamarine eyes sent a shaft of desire spearing through him. "I need to stay busy while you're gone, Lucius. Maybe if I fill every minute I won't miss you quite as much."

He cupped her face and feathered another kiss across her mouth. "Liar."

And she was a liar, Angie readily conceded the instant he left. Guilt threatened to overwhelm her at the way she'd set herself up as the "perfect" woman for Lucius. She would have been tempted to tell him the truth except for two vital facts. First, though she might not be "perfect"—who was?—she didn't have a single doubt that she suited him right down to the bones, just as he suited her. They fit together in every possible regard, from the way they related to one another, to emotional needs, to sexual compatibility. She'd never anticipated they'd bond so well, so fast.

But they had and she refused to feel guilt over one small lie if it forced Lucius to see what had been right under his nose all along.

Second, Mikey needed a mother, someone who would love him as much as she would her own child, love him in a way the Ridgeways would never offer due to what they perceived as the "stain" on his bloodline. Though she hadn't anticipated falling head over heels for a six-month-old, she had. And if it had taken one small lie to bring the three of them together as a family unit, well… She could live with the guilt. Besides, what did it matter how she and Lucius married, if the end result not only met their expectations, but exceeded them? Wasn't that the actual intent and purpose of the Pretorius Program?

She presented those same arguments over dinner at Trinity's apartment later that night. "Yeah, it sounds all nice and logical," her friend allowed. "But I have a feeling Devlin won't take your view of things. All he's going to see is a big, fat lie and hang you with it. You know he has trust issues. This isn't going to help him get over them."

Trinity pinpointed the one detail that continued to gnaw at Angie. "I keep hoping the ends justify the means," she muttered.

"A popular defense, but historically, it's one that tends to get people hanged." Trinity swept up their dinner plates and carted them into the kitchen. "I made cobbler. You want?"

"Did you make hard sauce to go with it?"

"Of course."

"Then I want."

Trinity laughed. "Just like my granny used to make with one small exception." She set a small dish of cobbler in front of Angie. "In addition to the butter and sugar, there's also a tablespoon of whiskey."

Angie stabbed a finger at her friend. "You're evil. I never noticed that about you before, but it's true."

"More like an evil genius. Since I don't hear you rejecting the offer, even with my small addition, I'll get the hard sauce."

Angie tucked Mikey more firmly in the crook of her arm and offered him another bite of the cooked carrots she'd brought for his dinner. He scrunched up his face and shoved the spoon away. "Got it. No more carrots. Dessert time, right? Give me a minute and I'll get your applesauce."

He didn't wait. Instead, he made a grab at her cobbler. Before she could whip it aside, he snatched up a small helping and shoved it into his mouth, crowing in approval at the flavor.

"The kid's got good taste," Trinity observed, setting a small bowl of hard sauce on the table.

Angie nipped her dessert plate clear of Mikey's reach. "The kid isn't allowed cobbler. He's too little. And make sure you keep that hard sauce on your side of the table. If the Ridgeways ever found out he ate something containing alcohol they'd slap Lucius with a lawsuit so fast they'd hear the sonic boom in the Antarctic."

Trinity obediently shifted the bowl. "So, when's the wedding and do I get to help pick out the dress?"

"This is Monday… The date's been set for a week from Friday."

"Nine days!" Trinity stared, nonplussed. "How are you supposed to pull everything together in nine days?"

"Apparently, Lucius has solved that problem by throwing money at it." Angie helped herself to a bite of cobbler. "One call and the invitations that couldn't possibly be ready for two weeks were available the same day. They go into the mail first thing tomorrow morning. The flowers have been ordered. Joe Milano is taking care of the cake. It's amazing how much you can accomplish in a single day when money is no object."

"What about a tux?"

Angie made a face. "Lucius must own a half-dozen tuxes, so that won't be a problem."

"Which leaves your wedding dress."

"Which is a problem," Angie acknowledged with a sigh.

"Not for long." Trinity dropped a generous dollop of hard sauce on her cobbler and dug in. "The day after tomorrow you, me and Mikey will hit the stores and we won't give up until we find the perfect gown. I'd drag you out shopping the first thing tomorrow—"

"But Mikey has his six-month checkup on Tuesday." Angie sighed. "Why don't you torture me instead of taking me shopping? It would be less painful."

Trinity shook her head, her expression turning serious. "You only have one first marriage, Ange. If you're lucky, only one marriage, period. You want it to be a day you'll remember for the rest of your life." She polished off the last of her cobbler and waved the purple-stained fork in Angie's direction. "And that means the perfect wedding dress."

Trinity was right, of course, and Angie couldn't explain her reluctance when it came to buying a gown. Maybe it went back to the feeling she'd cheated when it came to her marriage to Lucius. That because she'd asked Jett to alter the Pretorius Program, she'd manipulated him into marrying her. After putting an unusually cranky Mikey to bed for the night, she faced the unpalatable truth.

She wanted Lucius to marry her because he loved her, not for expedience.

Angie stood at the foot of the mile-wide bed—a cold and empty bed without Lucius—and struggled not to cry.

She'd made this bed. Time to lie in it. Based on their interactions to date, chances were excellent that it would be a good bed and a good marriage. She just needed to give them both time to develop their relationship a little more. To finish the process she didn't doubt they'd already started…and fall in love. Stripping off her clothes, she crawled beneath the covers. She missed Lucius. Missed him unbearably. Tugging his pillow into her arms, she buried her face in it. A faint trace of his scent clung to the fabric. Crisp and distinctly male with the merest hint of forest cedar.

She'd just started to drift off into a lovely dream that involved Lucius and a wedding in the clouds, when the phone on the bedside table rang. She rolled over to snatch it up before the sound woke Mikey. "Hello?"

"Did I wake you?" Lucius asked, his voice dark and rich, though she could hear the exhaustion running through his words.

"It's okay. I was just drifting off." She checked the clock, made the swift calculation between West Coast time and East and frowned. "What are you doing still up? It's nearly three in the morning."

"Just going over some last minute reports before turning in. I've been trying to sew everything up early, though it's not looking too encouraging."

Disappointment flooded through her and she struggled to keep the sound of it from filtering through her voice. "When will you be back?"

"Closer to the end of the week. Thursday, if I'm lucky, but I'm not sure if I can make it."

She plumped the pillows behind her and relaxed against them. "Where are you?" she asked.

His soft, knowing chuckle had her toes curling and sent shivers racing down her spine. "In bed. You?"

"The same."

"Ah… Give me a second to get an image." He released a sigh she'd only heard when they were both naked and he first slipped inside her. "Yes, there it is. What are you wearing?"

"Your pillow."

He groaned. "You're killing me."

"It smells like you, not that that's much help," she confessed. "I miss you."

"I miss you, too, sweetheart. It won't be much longer, I promise."

Silence settled between them, while the want grew thick. "Lucius…" she whispered.

"Me, too." He cleared his throat. "Okay, if we don't change the subject, I'm not going to get any sleep tonight. You…you remember Mikey has a checkup tomorrow?"

She strove to divorce herself emotionally, but it was far too late for that. Longing clung to her like Lucius's scent to his pillow. "Nine o'clock," she confirmed. "It's on the calendar."

"I wanted to be there for it. I almost postponed it a week, but it would have given the Ridgeways more ammunition to use against me."

"I'll take notes during the appointment. Fortunately, I'm really good at it."

"I appreciate it. You know that, don't you?"

"I do know." A plaintive cry came through the baby monitor beside the phone. "I think Mikey misses you, too."

"I hear him. Anything wrong?"

"He's just a little fussy tonight. Maybe he's cutting another tooth. Or maybe he knows I'm talking to you and wants his fair share of your attention."

"I know you have to go. Give me a quick update before you do. How are the wedding plans proceeding?"

"Good. Great, in fact. I think we have everything covered except for my dress. Trinity and I will be shopping for that on Wednesday." She released a sleepy laugh. "Technically, I guess that's tomorrow since it's now Tuesday morning."

"Get something beautiful. Money's no object."

"Lucius—"

He sighed. "Just do it, Angie. It's only money."

"Okay." There was so much more she wanted to say to him. So much she didn't dare. At least, not yet. "Mikey says I have to go now. Call me tomorrow?"

"I'll try." He hesitated, the words they both longed to speak hovering between them, hanging in the airwaves across the three thousand miles separating them. "Give our boy a hug from his… Aw, hell, from me. Good night, sweetheart."

"Good night, Lucius."

He couldn't say it, Angie realized. He still couldn't say the words he longed to. *Give our boy a hug from his daddy.* That's what he'd meant, what was in his heart. She could only hope that he'd soon be able to say them aloud putting words to the emotions he still denied.

She crossed to Mikey's bedroom and lifted him out of the crib. "Daddy says good-night, little guy. Is that why you're fussing? Because he wasn't here to tell you in person?"

Flipping on the overhead light, she carried him to the changing table. He blinked through his tears, his crying jag leaving his face red and blotchy. Or she assumed it was from the crying jag until she unsnapped his sleeper and saw that his face wasn't the only part of him all red and blotchy. Panicky fear swept through her. Something was wrong. Seriously wrong.

Scooping him up, she made a beeline for the kitchen

and the doctor's emergency number listed on the sheet taped to the refrigerator. She punched in the number, filled with relief when her call received an immediate answer, even though it was an answering service. The operator reassured her in a calm, soothing manner, promising the doctor would phone back within a minute or two. Sure enough, she'd no sooner hung up than the phone rang again.

"This is Dr. Graceland. Describe the symptoms," the pediatrician requested briskly. He listened, then asked, "Is Mikey having difficulty breathing?"

"No, not that I've noticed."

"Do you have a liquid antihistamine on hand, preferably dye-free?"

Holding the phone to her ear with her shoulder, she hurried to the medicine cabinet in the bathroom, found an unopened box and scanned the information. "Yes. Yes, I have it and it says it's dye-free."

After verifying age and weight, the doctor said, "Give the baby one quarter teaspoon. Wait half an hour and call me if there's no improvement. In the meantime, try a cool bath in case it's a reaction to something he's come into contact with physically, like pet hair or a new detergent. And make a list of everything he's eaten the past twenty-four hours."

"There's nothing he hasn't tried before," she started to say. Then remembered Mikey's grab for her cobbler. "Wait. He managed to get a handful of my cobbler at dinner."

"That's a possibility, particularly if it contained egg, dairy, nuts or wheat. Even more likely if one of his parents exhibited a similar allergy. Do you know of any allergies that run in the family?"

"I have no idea," she admitted. "Both his parents are deceased."

"Yes, of course. I remember now. Give him the antihistamine and if his symptoms don't improve, call me back and I'll meet you at the hospital. If they do improve, come into the office at eight and I'll bump you to the front of the line."

"Thank you, Dr. Graceland."

The next half hour felt like forever. A dozen different times she reached for the phone to call Lucius, each time resisting the urge. There wasn't anything he could do to help except worry. And he had enough to worry about without this. Besides, she could see an almost immediate improvement as soon as she administered the medication. It would have been a different story if she'd needed to rush the baby to the hospital.

It wasn't until she'd finished bathing and redressing Mikey that another thought occurred, one that shocked her to the core. This time she did snatch up the phone.

"Wha—?"

"Trinity, it's Angie."

"Wha—?"

"Look, I'm sorry it's so late, but it's important. Tell me what was in the cobbler we ate tonight."

Trinity groaned. "Are you kidding me? Do you have any idea what time I have to get up in the morning to go to work? You woke me because you couldn't wait a few more hours to get my recipe for cobbler?"

"No, I woke you because Mikey may have had an allergic reaction to your cobbler. What was in it?"

"Oh, hell." Her friend suddenly sounded more alert. "Okay, okay. Ingredients for cobbler. Um, sugar, blueberries, raspberries—"

"Currants? Did you use currants?"

Trinity gave a quick laugh of surprise. "As a matter of fact…"

"Thanks, that's all I needed to know."

"Wait, what—"

"I'll explain later. Go back to sleep."

Angie hung up without waiting for a response. Currants. If that turned out to be the cause of the allergic reaction, and the allergy ran in the family… Was it possible? Could Lucius actually be Mikey's father? She fought to think it through logically, to try and figure out her next step. If the two were father and son, how did she prove it? Another DNA test, obviously. But that would involve informing Lucius of her suspicions. She hated getting his hopes up only to have them dashed if she was wrong.

So, how did she work around that minor detail? Whenever faced with a new situation she didn't understand, she gathered facts. Researched. That was easy enough. She carried the baby to the computer and booted it up, then ran a fast search on DNA testing. To her relief, Mikey nodded off in her arms, the hives fading with each minute that ticked by.

"Well, look at that," she murmured. "I had no idea it was so easy. Or that you could do a home paternity test. Best of all, I can get the results by the time Lucius returns on Friday."

The website provided a long list of items from which they could extract DNA, examples of which she could find around the apartment without involving Lucius directly. She just had to pick one, send it in and wait for the results. And if the test results confirmed he fathered Mikey? She leaned back in the chair and cuddled the baby close. It would mean that Lisa had somehow falsified the results of Mikey's paternity test. Another thought struck. If she was right, Lucius wouldn't need her any longer because the Ridgeways would no longer have a viable claim on Mikey.

"Damn," she whispered. "What do I do now?"

There wasn't really any question about what she'd do. She'd let Lucius off the marital hook by ending their engagement gracefully and without complaint. Tears filled her eyes. Maybe, just maybe he wouldn't want to be let off the hook. Maybe he'd demand she stick to the agreement they'd made because he… She buried her head against Mikey's curls. Because he *what?* Because he wanted to be married to her? Because he *loved* her?

Foolish, foolish girl. Lucius had been up-front about what he wanted from the beginning. He'd offered marriage in order to ensure he retained guardianship of Mikey. Sure, he enjoyed the fringe benefits of their relationship. The companionship. The sex. A wife to take care of all the little wifely duties. But not once had he said anything about love. In fact, he'd gone out of his way to tell her he didn't think himself capable of that particular emotion. Was it his fault that she'd fallen head over heels for him?

She swept the back of her hand across her damp cheeks. Enough. She didn't even know if Lucius was Mikey's father. Once she'd settled that issue, she'd worry about the next step. In the meantime, she'd keep a close watch on Mikey in case he suffered a relapse from the allergen he'd come into contact with. And on Wednesday she'd choose a wedding gown, even knowing she may never wear it. She sighed.

Better make it returnable.

He didn't think Friday would ever arrive or that his meetings would ever come to an end. He boarded his private jet by noon, delighted he'd soon surprise Angie with an early arrival. He'd made a startling discovery during his five days in New York, one he'd tried for weeks to deny, but no longer could.

He'd fallen utterly, hopelessly, completely in love. And it wasn't with just one person, but two. His feelings for Mikey had been steadily growing, bit by bit, over the past three months until he had no choice but to concede that he flat-out loved the baby, had even come to regard Mikey as his own son. But his feelings for Angie hadn't crept up on him. They'd hit him with all the power and fury of a Cat 5 hurricane, flinging him into the midst of an inescapable storm of emotion.

He'd discovered something else during his trip to New York. He didn't just want Angie for the sake of his son—and Mikey was as much his son as Geoff had been his brother, Lucius now admitted. No, he wanted her in his life…for himself. A permanent part of that life. And the minute he saw her again, he intended to tell her so.

The only remaining question was… Could he convince Angie to change her mind, too? Could he convince her to give their marriage a chance, a real chance? To accept the ring on her finger as a sincere promise of intent, and the wedding they'd organized as the start of a true marriage.

His cell phone rang while they were waiting for permission for takeoff and he checked the caller ID. Pretorius St. John. Flipping open the phone, Lucius greeted the programmer. "How's it going, Pretorius?"

"To be honest? Not good."

"I'm sorry to hear that. How can I help?"

"It's not how you can help me. It's how I can help you." Pretorius sighed. "Listen, there's something you need to know about your 'perfect' wife-to-be. Unfortunately, it involves my former assistant, Jett."

Ten

Angie stood in front of the mirror and ran a trembling hand across the skirt of her wedding gown. She didn't think she'd ever seen anything more stunning in her life. It made her look…amazing. Beautiful. Elegant. Like some sort of storybook princess.

The pale ivory gown possessed an Empire waist and squared-off bodice, studded with Swarovski crystals and a skirt that fell in a straight column, the material so light and airy that it made her appear as though she were floating. Even with a flowing train, she found she could move without any problem.

She'd been experimenting with her hair to see what style best suited the classic lines of the gown, the decision easily made the second she'd pinned her curls into a loose knot on top of her head, allowing little tendrils to drift about her neck and temples.

"All you need is a tiara," came a voice from behind her.

Angie spun around with a gasp. "Lucius!"

"Surprise, surprise."

Why, oh why, had he chosen this particular moment to return? Fifteen minutes earlier and she wouldn't have yet donned the gown. Fifteen minutes later and she'd have finished trying it on and it would be safely tucked away in the closet. "You aren't supposed to see me in my wedding gown before the ceremony."

A small smile played at the corners of his mouth, one that caused a tremor of unease to shoot through her. "In our case, I don't think that's an issue," he said, the extreme gentleness of his tone causing her nervousness to increase. She knew that tone. It was a bad tone. A dangerous tone. One he used when he was about to take down one of his competitors.

Then his comment sank in. Seeing her in her wedding gown wasn't an issue for them because they weren't marrying for normal reasons, such as love. Perhaps that explained the tone. Why did she keep forgetting their marriage wasn't a real one, especially when she doubted the marriage would even take place? Ever since receiving the results from the DNA test this morning, results which proved with 99.99% certainty that Lucius was Mikey's father, she'd accepted the strong likelihood that next week's wedding ceremony would be the first casualty.

Angie had no idea how Lisa had manipulated the results in the first place. Perhaps she'd faked the test from the get-go, hiring actors to play the part of technicians. Or perhaps she'd paid one of the technicians to falsify the results at whatever lab they'd used. Or maybe it was a simple clerical error, the lab accidentally switching samples by mistake. All that mattered was that Lucius now had enough probable cause to have another test done, one that would hold up in a court of law.

Which meant…he wouldn't need to marry.

Which meant…she stood before him in a wedding gown she'd never use, at least not for its intended purpose.

Oh, what did it matter? "You're right, of course. It's not an issue for us." Angie started toward Lucius, her hands held out, a smile of sheer delight spilling free. "I'm so glad you're home early."

"Are you? Are you really?"

The barely audible questions contained an unmistakable bite and dismay swamped her, checking her forward momentum. She hesitated in the middle of the room, filled with uncertainty. Her arms slowly fell to her sides. What in the world was going on? "I…I should change," she murmured. Because whatever was wrong, she'd rather not deal with it while wearing a wedding gown.

"Don't. I think I'd prefer having this conversation with you dressed just as you are."

She stilled. Something was off, seriously off. She'd suspected it when he first spoke. Now she didn't have a single doubt. "Lucius? What's going on?"

"An excellent question. Perhaps you could answer it for me."

She shook her head, feeling the curls around her neck dance in agitation. "I don't understand. Is something wrong?"

"Yes, Angie. Something is wrong. Something is very wrong." He approached. Circled. "I don't think I've ever seen you look more beautiful. Not at all like office furniture. You've certainly come up in the world this past month."

Her chest felt as though it were squeezed in a vise, and her breath came swift and shallow in response. Every instinct she possessed compelled her to run. Instead, she could only stand, frozen in place, while he circled, circled,

circled. She caught a brief glimpse of herself in the mirror, saw the crystal beads fracture beneath the overhead light, shooting shards of desperate color into the room and realized it was because she was trembling.

"That should sound like a compliment." She moistened her lips. "Why doesn't it sound like a compliment, Lucius?"

"Do you know, I never saw it coming. I really have to applaud you. I'm not easily fooled, but I must say you played your part exceptionally well. Better even than Lisa."

Oh, God, he knew. Somehow he'd found out that she and Jett manipulated the Pretorius Program. "Lucius, I can explain—"

He stopped his endless circling, pausing in front of her, and what she read in his face eviscerated her. She'd never seen such ruthless intent. Instead of fury, as she would have expected, she saw that he'd encased himself in ice, staring at her from eyes so cold and remote and deadly she didn't have a chance in hell of ever getting through to him. That didn't change the fact that she needed to try.

Before she could begin an explanation, he spoke again. "Seriously, Angie. I'm impressed. I really am. I've worked with you on a daily basis for eighteen months. And not once, not one single time, did you deviate from your role. That's truly an amazing feat. Very difficult to sustain, long-term. And I must say that choosing suits to match my office furniture was probably the coup de grâce. A stroke of brilliance. It was the final detail that sold the entire scam." He slowly clapped his hands. If the sound of clapping could be described as sarcastic, he'd perfected a sarcastic clap. "Brava, Angie."

"You know about the Pretorius Program."

He smiled in genuine amusement. "Why, yes. I do know."

She swallowed past the thickness clogging her throat. "How…?"

"Pretorius discovered Jett tampered with the results. As soon as he put it together, he called me." He folded his arms across his chest, stretching the fabric of his black suit across the impressive width of his shoulders, underscoring the sheer physical strength and power of the man. "I'm curious… I assume when you accepted the position of PA you hoped the job would eventually transition into that of my wife. How would you have attempted to trick me into marriage if I hadn't been foolish enough to offer you the perfect opportunity with the Pretorius Program?"

She couldn't control the soft laugh that bubbled free at the bizarre turn the conversation had taken. "Oh, gosh, let me count the ways. Maybe I'd have done a striptease on your desk. Gotten accidentally pregnant. Found some deep, dark secret hidden away in your files and blackmailed you into marriage. I'm sure I would have come up with something."

"None of those things would have worked. Not on me."

She blinked. Good grief, he actually believed her. "Well, damn, Lucius. Now I'm really disappointed, because God knows marrying you just has to be the ultimate goal of every woman in Seattle. Maybe in the entire Northwest." She snapped her fingers. "Maybe even in the whole of the good ol' U.S. of A."

"You think this is funny?"

His voice flicked like a lash, cutting painfully, and she flinched. "Not even a little. Explain something, Lucius. Why are you so angry? I thought you wanted a wife. What difference does it make how you got one if she fulfills your requirements?"

"But you don't fulfill my requirements. You lied about your abilities. Pretorius discovered that, as well."

She released a sigh. "True enough. I did lie. Though if you don't mind my saying, they were ridiculous requirements."

"That's not for you to decide!"

"Oh, right." She planted her hands on her hips, her anger rising to meet his, exceeding it. "And we both know how well those requirements were working before I agreed to marry you, don't we? How many women did you go through, Lucius? How many of them told you to go to hell like Ella? Do you think you'd have found someone else by now, your *perfect* wife, if I hadn't stepped in?"

"How the hell do I know? Maybe she would have been the next name on the list."

"And maybe she doesn't exist." Angie ticked off on her fingers. "A gourmet cook. A superb housekeeper. An excellent interior designer. A mother. A wife with fringe benefits. Come on. Are you kidding me?"

A hint of color swept across the arch of his cheekbones. "Those aren't unreasonable requirements."

She swept them aside with a wave of her hand. "They're ridiculous requirements. The only important ones, the only ones you should have been focused on were acquiring a wife who would love and care for Mikey and who would—" She broke off, her throat closing over, preventing her from finishing her statement. She stood in front of him, utterly exposed, aware he'd have no problem deducing the rest of her comment. *...and who would love and care for you.*

He shook his head, fury melting through the ice and burning across his expression. "Don't. Don't try and turn this into some sort of grand romance. What we shared was purely physical. Sex and nothing more. Our marriage is for Mikey's sake, not for any other reason. Are we clear on that point?"

"Crystal." She tugged off the engagement ring and held it out to him.

He took her wrist in an unbreakable hold and thrust the ring back on her finger. "Our engagement doesn't end until I say it does. You will marry me, Angie. Only now you'll do it on my terms, as per our contract."

"That's where you're wrong, Lucius." She didn't attempt to pull free. She simply met his gaze head-on, refusing to back down. "The gown is returnable. I haven't mailed out the invitations. Both the floral shop and Joe Milano have been called and instructed to put the flowers and reception dinner on hold. The Dorchester Chapel is also on hold pending your phone call to either move forward with the ceremony or cancel."

He stared at her a full thirty seconds, his black eyes narrowed in assessment. She could practically see him picking his way through the information, searching for the catch, struggling to evaluate what advantage canceling the wedding gave her. "You work for the Ridgeways," he finally said. "It's the only explanation. String me along, get inside information on me and then back out of our wedding right before they hit me with a lawsuit. Stand up in court and tell the judge about the Pretorius Program and my attempts to buy myself a wife. Custody of Mikey goes to the Ridgeways. End of game."

She couldn't help herself. She laughed. It was either that or burst into tears. "There are times you break my heart, Lucius."

"What other explanation could there be?"

"An excellent question. Let go of my wrist, please."

She continued to hold his gaze until he complied. And then she removed the ring for a second time. Instead of handing it to him, she crossed to his dresser and placed it dead center on the gleaming wood. The fire diamond flashed in reaction, sending out rays of hope that faded with each passing moment, along with a promise that would never be kept.

Angie glanced over her shoulder at Lucius. "Would you mind unbuttoning me? I had so much trouble getting it buttoned, it'll take me all night before I can change back into my office furniture."

Without a word, he approached. He released the column of tiny crystal buttons one by one, his fingers skimming the length of her spine. She fought to conceal her shiver of reaction, fought harder to divorce herself from the emotions clamoring for release. His warmth caressed her back and she gripped the edge of the dresser in an effort to steady herself. He swept the dress from her shoulders, baring her to the waist.

She wore a bra with barely-there cups specifically designed to work with the bodice of the dress, one that took what little she had and made it appear… Well, if not impressive, at least adequate. Based on Lucius's reaction, possibly more than adequate. Angie caught the change in his breathing, the subtle catching hitch followed by a deep, dragging inhale. Bending forward slightly, she allowed the dress to drift toward the floor to pool at her feet in a puddle of ivory silk tears.

She'd hoped—how she'd hoped—they would be married by the time Lucius saw her in the delicate undergarments. The soft bridal ivory of the scraps of silk and lace matched her gown and were held together with tiny bows that coyly promised, with one gentle tug, to bare her to his gaze. She stepped free of the gown, fully aware of how she appeared in heels, garter and stockings. Let him look, she decided. Let him get a good, long look…and regret.

Ever so gently, Angie gathered up the gown and carried it to the closet, replacing it in the protective bag the shop had provided. She continued to ignore him, removing one of her older suits from its hanger, the outfit he'd once upon a time compared to chair upholstery. She started to dress, but before she could do more than reach for the skirt, Lucius stopped her.

"Don't."

He turned her around to face him. For a split second the barriers between them fell and he swept her into his arms, his fingers forking deep into her hair, loosening the topknot. And then he consumed her. The kiss held endless passion, combined with an underlying anger and hurt. She could taste his pain, his disillusionment, and tears filled her eyes.

One last time. For this brief moment, she'd take whatever he offered. Take it and imprint it on her memory so in the painful days to come, she could slip it out and remember. Just one last time.

Her lips parted beneath his and he swept inward, taking her. Marking her. Telling her with his kiss what he didn't dare say aloud. He loved her. She didn't have a single doubt in her mind, just as she didn't have a single doubt that their love was doomed. He didn't trust. Couldn't. Not that she blamed him. She'd lied. Broken faith with him, which was the one thing he couldn't forgive.

"Why?" he demanded against her mouth, the question escaping between deep, passionate kisses. "Why would you betray me like this?"

The tears escaped despite her best efforts to control them. "It's not a betrayal. I swear it isn't."

"It can't be anything else. Not when you lied to me. Not when you pretended to be something you aren't."

Her laugh splintered on heartbreak. "I never pretended

to be anything other than I am. You were the one looking for the perfect wife. What you don't realize is you ended up with someone who's more than perfect…at least for you. Don't throw it away now."

But he was already pulling back, shaking his head. He stepped clear of her and tossed her suit into her arms. "Get dressed. Then we'll discuss where we go from here." With that, Lucius turned on his heel and left the bedroom.

Angie pulled on her clothing without a word, not bothering to change out of her wedding undergarments. Pointless now since they'd never be used for a wedding. She took a final look around, attempting to determine if there was anything too urgent to leave behind. There wasn't. Just one final stop before she left the apartment, left behind the life she'd hoped to build here.

She walked into Mikey's room and found him batting at dust motes, having just woken from his nap. "Hey, there, little guy," she greeted in a soft voice. She lifted him from his crib and cradled him close, tears clogging her throat. "You have no idea how much I'm going to miss you."

He smelled of sweet, clean baby with a hint of powder. He grabbed the loosened tendrils of her hair and tugged them toward his mouth. She untangled her hair from his chubby fist with a tearful laugh. He was so beautiful. Had managed to become such a vital part of her life. She didn't think she'd ever recover from the loss of both Mikey and Lucius, the two men she'd come to love with all her heart.

"I tried. At least I tried," she whispered against the top of Mikey's head. "I thought I'd be… I wanted to be… Oh, Mikey, I'd hoped I'd be your mother. To care for you. Nurture you. Watch you grow to manhood." She held him for endless minutes, absorbing his baby warmth, his baby scent, the quick, eager heartbeat thumping against her breast. "I love you. I'll always love you."

She needed to go. A quick, decisive end to it before she lost control, altogether. She carried Mikey into the living room. Lucius stood in front of the bank of windows overlooking the city, the light streaming behind him settling on her and the baby, while framing him in darkness. It was a calculated maneuver, one she'd seen him use before. She negated his advantage by crossing to his side and settling the son in the father's arms. Now that she knew the truth, it seemed so obvious. The set of the eyes, the curve of the mouth, that stubborn, authoritative chin, one a miniaturized mirror of the other.

"Before we take this any further I want to know, once and for all, whether you're working with the Ridgeways," Lucius announced, taking immediate charge. Devil Devlin at his most intimidating.

She released a distracted sigh, glancing around for her purse. She spotted it on the couch and retrieved it. Then she walked to the foyer and stabbed the call button for the elevator.

"Where the hell do you think you're going? Don't you even think of walking out on me, Angie." He took a step in her direction, seemed to suddenly realize that holding Mikey in his arms prevented him from physically stopping her. Frustration bloomed across his face. "You aren't leaving until you explain why you did this."

"Actually, Lucius, you should already know why I did this. You asked often enough." The door slid silently open and she stepped into the car. Turning, she pushed one of the buttons on the panel. "You just never listened to my answer."

And with that, the door closed between them.

Lucius glared at the elevator doors. "How am I supposed to hear something she never said?" he demanded of Mikey. "If she thinks this is the end of it, she's about to learn otherwise."

Mikey leaned in the direction of the elevator and held out his arms, making clear his displeasure at Angie's disappearance.

"You and me both," Lucius muttered.

He continued to bore holes through the elevator doors as though they held all the answers to the universe and were deliberately keeping them from him. Ever since the call from Pretorius, Lucius had stewed over what Angie had done, the coast-to-coast flight providing him with all the time in the world to first whip himself into a full-blown, brain-melting, self-righteous rage, before chilling into the sort of bitter cold reserve he'd perfected ever since Lisa's marriage to Geoff. It had been his only defense during that bleak time.

When he and Angie had first made their devil's bargain, somehow, someway, she'd managed to release him from that. How had it happened? *When* had it happened? Without him even being fully aware of it, she'd infiltrated his life, knocking down barriers, easing that long, lean glorious body of hers into every aspect of his world, even the private corners where she didn't belong. He closed his eyes. Where she'd become so damn necessary. Vital. Needed. Oh, *hell.* Where he'd fallen in love with her and slowly—like a tender shoot shoving its way through an earth still half-frozen from winter's barren chill—ever so slowly, come alive again.

Which only made her betrayal all the more cutting. Then he'd arrived home and found her in a wedding dress. God in heaven. She'd been breathtaking. Radiant. And the expression on her face… It had been that of a woman caught in a moment of perfect happiness. Until he'd stolen that moment from her. Until he'd stripped her of the dream the way she'd stripped herself of her wedding gown. And if the sight of her in that gown had threatened to bring him to his knees, it didn't begin to compare to what he'd experienced seeing her in those filmy bits of ivory, barely held together with satin bows of promise. Bows he'd have given anything to untie, one by one by everlasting one.

Frustration welled up inside. "Damn it, if she didn't betray me, why didn't she stay? Why didn't she fight?"

There had to be a reason and the only one he came up with was that he'd been right about her working for the Ridgeways. And yet… Now that he'd had more time to reflect, seen the quiet pain and hurt anger of her response—or lack of response—it simply didn't add up. He blew out a sigh. Mikey glanced up at him and babbled out a question.

"Yeah, we're going after her. And this time we're not leaving until she tells us why she had Jett set her up as my perfect wife. And then there will be bows to untie." He gave Mikey a man-to-man look. "That's a bit like hell to pay, only a lot more fun."

He snatched up Mikey's diaper bag, intent on giving chase and that's when he saw the envelope poking out of one of the zippered pockets, his name neatly scripted across the outside. He instantly recognized Angie's handwriting. Finally. An explanation.

"Let's hear what she has to say for herself." He slid a hip on the arm of the couch, tucked Mikey more securely into the crook of one arm and opened the envelope. It took him almost a full minute to process the information. "Oh, God."

The test results drifted from his grasp and his second arm wrapped solidly around Mikey. Around *his son.* He reached out a trembling hand, stroking it along Mikey's downy cheek, his black gaze locking with an equally black gaze. He had a son. All this time, Mikey was his and he never knew. Never even suspected, not after that initial paternity test. Worst of all, he'd had his son in his life for a full three months and refused to allow himself to get too close, to open himself up to the bond steadily growing between them. And why?

Fear.

Fear of abandonment. Fear of giving himself over to love. Fear of losing control.

Fear of allowing another person in, a person who could hurt him, compromise him emotionally.

He closed his eyes. How close had he come to losing his son? If the Ridgeways had won custody of Mikey would it even have occurred to him to demand a second paternity test? Highly doubtful. If it hadn't been for Angie…

He slowly straightened. Angie. How the bloody hell had she known? And how had she gotten a sample of his DNA to have tested in the first place? If Mikey truly was his son and she'd figured out what no one else had, then it didn't make sense that she was in the employ of the Ridgeways. Nothing made any sense anymore. Only one person possessed the answers he required.

Angie. He needed to find Angie.

It had been an endless night, one in which Angie had gotten next to no sleep. She'd returned home after her fight with Lucius, not quite certain what to do with herself in the little cottage that was her home, and yet, wasn't anymore.

She'd wandered from room to room while minutes ticked into hours and evening transitioned to night. Little by little, she realized Lucius wouldn't come. Night deepened into that still, dense time where hope slipped away while fears gathered and wandered freely. And still he didn't come. Not until dawn chased away the darkness that seemed to have seeped into the walls and furnishings, into the very pores of the house, did Angie finally fall asleep on the couch, curled into a tight ball, an afghan wrapped around her for warmth and comfort.

And that's where he found her.

She woke to Mikey's demanding cry, groggy and confused. "I'll get him," she muttered, her eyes refusing to unglue themselves. What in the world had happened to their bed? It felt like someone had filled it with rocks during the night. She yawned. "Probably needs his diaper changed."

"Not really. I think he just needs his mother."

Dishes rattled nearby and she caught the subtle fragrance of her favorite tea. Memory slammed through her. Lucius. Mikey. The Pretorius Program. Oh, God, their fight. Her eyes popped open, fighting to focus through the blur of a sleepless night and too many tears.

And there was Lucius, crouched beside her, steam wafting from the translucent porcelain cup and saucer he held. Mikey sat at his feet in a carrier, pumping his little arms and legs as though trying to swim through the air in order to reach her.

"What…?" She struggled to get her brain cells to fire. "How…? How did you get in?"

"You left the front door unlocked—an oversight we'll discuss later. So, I made myself at home." He handed her the tea. "Drink."

She'd have refused, just on sheer principle, but the tea smelled too delicious. Plus, if she had a hope in hell of dealing with Lucius, she'd better get some caffeine in her. She took a restorative sip and nearly moaned. Or maybe she did. For some reason, the sound caused Lucius's eyes to flare. Once upon a time she'd have said it was passion. Not anymore. Not considering how they'd parted.

She sat up, painfully aware she only wore a thin nightgown. Great. Just great. Could she be at any more of a disadvantage? She took another sip of tea before shoving her hair out of her face. And then she forced herself to meet his gaze. He continued to crouch in front of her, which put him far too close for comfort.

"Why are you here, Lucius?" she asked, seizing the offense. "If it's to make more accusations—"

"I'm here to apologize."

"And I've already told you…" Wait. What? "Did you say *apologize?*"

"Yes." A smile twitched at the corners of his mouth, though he answered gravely enough. "I'm sorry, Angie. I should have trusted you. I should have known that even if you and Jett did put your heads together in order to manipulate the Pretorius Program, it was with the best of intentions."

Angie scrubbed trembling hands across her face. "Either I'm dreaming or…" She shook her head, struggling to focus through the pain and fatigue. "I can't think of an or," she admitted in a heartbreaking voice.

"You're not dreaming. I'm really here. And I'm really apologizing, most sincerely apologizing."

Tears burned her eyes and throat. "Don't," she begged. "Don't do this to me. Not unless you really mean it. I can't bear—"

The sound of her broken plea proved too much for him and he swept her off the couch and into his arms. He cupped her face, took her mouth in a soft, tender kiss. "I love you. And I'm sorry."

"Sorry you love me?"

He laughed softly. "I can never be sorry for that, regardless of your feelings for me. You gave me my son. A son I'd never have known I possessed if not for you."

"Oh, Lucius." She burrowed against him. "Why didn't you come last night? I hoped you would. I waited and waited and you never showed up."

"I had a stop I needed to make first. It took me longer than expected."

Her head jerked upward. "The Ridgeways?" At his nod, she asked, "How did they take the news?"

"They demanded another DNA test. I agreed, of course. But I could tell they believed me, and it devastated them." His mouth tightened. "It devastated them at first. Then they demanded I reimburse them for all the expenses they'd incurred while taking care of Mikey over the course of the past three months."

"Oh, Lucius."

His eyes went stark. "I wrote them out a check then and there."

She hesitated. "So… What now?"

"Now we talk. Now we're totally honest with one another, starting with… Why did you change the Pretorius Program? Why did you agree to marry me?"

She remained silent. And waited. Hope crept into her heart and took root there, which terrified her. What if she were mistaken? She didn't think she could handle it if he got this part wrong. She didn't have to wait for long.

"You agreed to marry me because you love me."

He made the statement with an absolute certainty that devastated her. She closed her eyes and allowed the words to wash over and through her. To fill her to overflowing. It took three tries to respond. "Yes, Lucius. I agreed to marry you because I love you, and for no other reason. I've loved you almost since I first came to work for you."

"And I've been an ignorant ass almost since you first came to work for me."

She smiled, her smile growing to a grin. "I won't argue with that."

"I'm sorry, Angie. I should have trusted you."

"I did lie to you. And collude with Jett. But I hoped that someday you'd feel what I've felt all this time and realize what I've realized."

"Which is?"

She cupped his face and feathered a kiss across his mouth. "Why, that I'm the perfect woman for you, Lucius Devlin."

He reached into his pocket and removed the engagement ring she'd left behind. Taking her hand in his, he returned it to her finger where it belonged. Where it would remain forevermore. Where soon, he hoped, it would be joined by a wedding band. And then he kissed her, kissed her in a way that left her in no doubt that he loved her. Would always love her. That she was his, just as he was hers. At their feet, Mikey crowed in delight, putting his stamp of approval on the relationship.

When Lucius finally surfaced, he gazed down at her. The shadows were gone, the final barriers fallen. What remained, the love and certainty that solidified there, belonged to her and no one else. Well, except for their son, of course.

"You're wrong, you know. You're not the perfect woman for me," Lucius informed her. "You are, and always will be, more than perfect."

Epilogue

Lucius and Angie married as planned, taking their vows just as the sun set against the snowcapped peaks of the Olympic Mountains.

The bride looked like a princess in an ivory gown studded with Swarovski crystals over delicate undergarments held together with dainty bows the groom looked forward to untying later that evening. She also wore the bridal gift he'd surprised her with—a bracelet, earrings and necklace—and, of course, her engagement ring.

No one present doubted theirs was a love match. If the guests found it strange that the couple promised to love, honor and always be truthful with one another, they dismissed it as a mild and acceptable eccentricity of the very wealthy. Nor did they doubt how much the couple adored the baby the groom held in his arms throughout most of the ceremony, only relieved of his precious burden when the time came to kiss his bride.

And during that first kiss between husband and wife, the fire diamonds she wore seemed to capture the light of the fading sun, sending a blaze of fire shooting through the room, a magical flame filled with love's promise.

Everyone in attendance agreed.

It was all…Utter Perfection.

* * * * *

PASSION

For a spicier, decidedly hotter read—
this is your destination for romance!

COMING NEXT MONTH

AVAILABLE MARCH 13, 2012

#2143 TEMPTED BY HER INNOCENT KISS
Pregnancy & Passion
Maya Banks

#2144 BEHIND BOARDROOM DOORS
Dynasties: The Kincaids
Jennifer Lewis

#2145 THE PATERNITY PROPOSITION
Billionaires and Babies
Merline Lovelace

#2146 A TOUCH OF PERSUASION
The Men of Wolff Mountain
Janice Maynard

#2147 A FORBIDDEN AFFAIR
The Master Vintners
Yvonne Lindsay

#2148 CAUGHT IN THE SPOTLIGHT
Jules Bennett

There came a time in a man's life when he knew he was well and truly caught. Devon Carter stared down at the diamond ring nestled in velvet and acknowledged that this was one such time. He snapped the lid closed and shoved the box into the breast pocket of his suit.

He had two choices. He could marry Ashley Copeland and fulfill his goal of merging his company with Copeland Hotels, thus creating the largest, most exclusive line of resorts in the world, or he could refuse and lose it all.

Put in that light, there wasn't much he could do except pop the question.

The doorman to his Manhattan high-rise apartment hurried to open the door as Devon strode toward the street. He took a deep breath before ducking into his car, and the driver pulled into traffic.

Tonight was the night. All of his careful wooing, the countless dinners, kisses that started brief and casual and became more breathless—all a lead-up to tonight. Tonight his seduction of Ashley Copeland would be complete, and then he'd ask her to marry him.

He shook his head as the absurdity of the situation hit him for the hundredth time. Personally, he thought William Copeland was crazy for forcing his daughter down Devon's throat.

Ashley was a sweet enough girl, but Devon had no desire

HDEXP0312

to marry anyone.

William had other plans. He'd told Devon that Ashley had no head for the family business. She was too softhearted, too naive. So he'd made Ashley part of the deal. The catch? Ashley wasn't to know of it. Which meant Devon was stuck playing stupid games.

Ashley was supposed to think this was a grand love match. She was a starry-eyed woman who preferred her animal-rescue foundation over board meetings, charts and financials for Copeland Hotels.

If she ever found out the truth, she wouldn't take it well.

And hell, he couldn't blame her.

But no matter the reason for his proposal, before the night was over, she'd have no doubts that she belonged to him.

What will happen when Devon marries Ashley?
Find out in Maya Banks's passionate new novel
TEMPTED BY HER INNOCENT KISS
Available March 2012 from Harlequin Desire!

HDEXP0312